I'VE SEEN THE YELLOW CRANE

我见过黄鹤

张执浩 著　　何跃敏 译

By Zhang Zhihao

Translated by He Yuemin

外文出版社
FOREIGN LANGUAGES PRESS

First Edition 2024

ISBN 978-7-119-14025-4

Published by Foreign Languages Press Co. Ltd
24 Baiwanzhuang Road, Beijing 100037, China
Distributed by China International Book Trading Corporation
35 Chegongzhuang Xilu, Beijing 100044, China
P.O. Box 399, Beijing, China

Printed in the People's Republic of China

译者序言

《我见过黄鹤》是即将陆续出版的汉英对照“武汉作家作品译介”丛书中的第一部。这套丛书体裁广泛，风格各异，包括武汉著名现当代作家的选作。

本书收录 183 首诗，主要选自诗人张执浩的诗集《高原上的野花》和《万古烧》。这些诗细心感受日常生活，抽丝剥茧地厘清街头巷尾、晚霞晨光里的波澜起伏，并通过贴切而非凡的诗歌语言表达出来。它把原本平常的人生经历转化为诗意的内容、鲜活的意象、亲切的心灵触摸，让读者在阅读中仿佛亲身经历滋滋冒着热气的青葱岁月、宽阔的江汉平原、容纳众生的胸怀、薪火相传的历程。它构建和传达的是一种对武汉和周边城乡的柔情，对生于斯长于斯的长江汉水的挚爱，对远亲近邻的友好呼唤。如果说一本书可以是一座城市，这座城市就是诗人用文字一砖一瓦构建出来的家国情怀。作为译者，我很高兴有缘斯人，有力气把这座城市通过这本书介绍给喜欢诗歌并通过诗歌来了解这座城市的读者们。

PREFACE

I Have Seen the Yellow Crane is the first book of the Chinese-English "Wuhan Poetry and Prose in Translation" series. This series presents selected works by the most prominent modern and contemporary Wuhan authors. The books cover various subjects and are distinguished in their respective styles.

Featuring 183 poems, selected mainly from *Wild Flowers on the Plateau* and *The Everlasting Pot* by contemporary Chinese poet Zhang Zhihao, *I Have Seen the Yellow Crane* showcases the poet's remarkable ability to stay close with daily life. It unravels the subtlest meanings from trivial happenings in the streets and alleys and the natural world, and then conveys them in an extraordinary poetic language. It transforms quotidian realities into poetic subject matter, vivid images, and highly relatable spiritual feelings. Ultimately, it offers the readers a vicarious experience of sizzling youth, the wide Jiang Han Plain, capacious understanding of the multitudes, and relay of valuable human traditions. Emanating a tender feeling for the city of Wuhan and its suburban neighborhoods, palpable passionate love of the Yangtze River as home and hearth, and generous kindness to friends nearby and afar, this book is a city in and of itself, words its bricks and love its mortar. As the translator, I feel great joy in translating these poems and sharing them with poetry lovers who are interested in accessing this city, real and literary.

INTRODUCTION

I started to read Zhang Zhihao's poetry while a friend and I were looking for poems to translate for entertainment, but once read, I could not have enough of it. Zhang's poetry is simply enjoyable with its eloquence, elegance, and elevating power. During the past three years, I turned to examining it with the more professional eyes of a translator, cultural studies specialist, and college educator. This volume of poetry translation is therefore a labor of love. Wearing three hats, I aim to share a delightful poetry experience with readers who love poetry for what it is and to help expand the global landscape of contemporary Chinese poetry.

(1)

Zhang's poetry is very eloquent. With a minimal repository of poetic techniques—metaphor, symbolism, parallel structure, personification, pun—it covers all sorts of subject matter in a remarkably accessible manner. Whether writing about the cityscape or countryside, current state of being or erstwhile Chinese common people's experiences, the personal or the public, Zhang's poetry comes with a magic sheen that adheres to "whatever the eyes see is poetry 目击成诗," which *Du Yi*《杜臆》, a famous literary commentary, used to characterize poetry by Du Fu who is one of the most influential Chinese poets ever. Zhang strives to turn out poetry that can speak to the core of the common, quotidian, and visceral.

More specifically, Zhang believes in the axiom, "Write what you know." He values truth and embraces truth even as it is beyond grasp, and if he cannot tell it, he decides not to lie. He accomplishes this by closely observing the smallest of life's details and distilling them for meaning. He insists these are the very moments that do matter—small pieces of daily living that define people and connect people as human beings.

For instance, in "A Steelyard" (一杆秤 See page 66), Zhang delineates a countryside afternoon he experienced and transforms it into an enlightening reading. Apparently, the villagers gathered to slaughter a buffalo for celebration because they were surrounding a giant boiling cauldron "in high spirits." The stars, measurement marks on the scale, were too greasy or illegible to read suggesting this slaughtering was a common practice. Since "I" narrate the story and "I" position "us" as apart from the rest of the villagers, "we" are likely children. It is just because of this innocence, the poem leads to the cutting truth: The scale was used to weigh how much buffalo meat there would be and how much meat each of the villagers would have. Therefore, the fact that "I" was on the hook and being weighed suddenly enabled "I" to at least momentarily empathize with the poor buffalo that was to be sacrificed. In addition, the Chinese phrase "斤两," which means one's worth, enables "me" to question "my" own worth or to realize "my" own insignificance and vulnerability. Ultimately, Zhang uses this poem to ask human beings to stoop down to the level of the buffalo to understand the other creatures' sacrifice and reexamine human assumptions and hubris. On the scale is not only bodily weight but also human lack of self-understanding.

Zhang grew up in the countryside. His knowledge of the countryside or everyday life of the country folks helps his poetry writing in detail, giving it a quirky twist to tone and style. It shapes Zhang's own content and thought to grow on that content, which forms a significant part of his poetry. It is no surprise to see him use planting rice seedlings as a vehicle for his poetics.

"Left Align" (左对齐 See page 4) portrays the poetry composition process, from a blank piece of paper to a page full of human characters, unfolding story, and eventual interior sensation. The extended metaphor—composing poetry is like transplanting rice seedlings in a field—is both picturesque and dynamic; visual and cerebral; sensual and analytical; and familiar and freshly new. It's hardly imaginable somebody who has never experienced that life would write in such surgical precision and yet with such poetic sensuality.

These poems reassure readers that daily life, whether hard or happy, is precious and meaningful if people contemplate it observantly. And it does it in a strikingly elegant manner. Zhang has fashioned a poetic voice of his own. He excels at a sound register ranging from the medium to the low. This sound register is characterized, as Zhang relates in "Poetry and Sound Register," by shunning exaggerated high-sounding tone and words, such as destiny, human society, nation, times, history, etc. His is a poetic voice that refuses to budge to the pretentious, spectacular trend, or yield to self-desire. He chooses to be deliberate, as Ralph Waldo Emerson believed that Man Thinking should.

For instance, it cannot be said that "In Response to My Love, to the New Year as Well" (答枕边人，兼致新年 See page 160) does not contain barbs, but the language register and tone of the poem sound so gentle and intimate that the poem flows almost like a lyrical love poem. The poem considers it miraculous to stay to the "original intention" and consoling to have days free of "smog." Readers easily read the poem as a social critique, or gentle buttering up, which means some built-in ambiguities. The language used is low-key, personal, and familiar. A poem like this sits well with general readers as it provokes thoughts and empathy with the speaker. The speaker finds it lucky to have survived it all with "you" at year's end. This feeling is highly relatable and intimate. There is no intricate poetry form, glaring technical somersaults, high-flown diction, and pretentious piety or insincerity; the poem simply speaks gently to the heart and lingers with a long finish, creating a delightful image of beauty.

Zhang is in truth very adroit with image creation. In "Conveyor Belt" (传送带 See page 53) he focuses on one who is waiting at the airport baggage carousel. Anyone who has taken a plane or long-distance bus, waited for a loved one, or experienced life in a similar manner, could relate to this hope, or yearning, the speaker conveys. In a world where increasingly people decline personal relationships to wrap themselves in technology, this poem can transport readers quickly back to beautiful old-fashioned sentiments. Zhang achieves this effect by comparing waiting for one's loved one to waiting for luggage at the carousel, and comparing the patience and commitment needed for nourishing a loving relationship to those needed for successful baggage claim. While using this metaphor, he is doubly engaged—the visual denotation and the emotional connotation. More than one thing is happening at once, and he invites the readers to respond at both levels. Zhang relishes the fun of playing with the purported meaning though he is mainly concerned with the second meaning of his poem. The resulting image is vivid, delightful, and easily identifiable.

Zhang's poetry is also effective in elevating the heart and mind to the most touching, daring, and far-reaching. For example, in "The Mushroom Spoke, and the Wood Ear Listened" (蘑菇说，木耳听 See page 46) the main literary device is personification, but the poem is humorous and profound. Evidently, the two characters cannot get along with each other despite their shared desire to return to where they grew up. The poem lends itself to many interpretations–racism, prejudice against people due to their weight, lack of dialogue, inability to return, mutual foible, etc., and it can thereby appeal to many different audiences.

"Hoop Rolling" (滚铁环 See page 54) is another poem that evokes children's innocence, but subtly morphs into awareness of the abysmal, difficult to grasp world. The poem presents a vignette of a countryside milieu: threshing ground, resting parents, and a child playing with an old bike tire. The poem begins with the child wide-eyed with amazement. But added into the mix are strains on the farmers—busy harvest time, hot weather, and exhausting field labor. The most unexpected looms large near the end where the child runs at high speed into thicker and thicker darkness. The early strains are nothing compared with this imperious darkness. In 15 lines, the poem turns one late evening into a symbol of unfathomable precarity of life while youthful in tone.

As shown, although these poems may appear to be about the routine, personal, and even insignificant, they not only penetrate deep into the essence of life and human circumstances but also elevate the mind to where readers can sustain through the day, spot beauty in the simple, and aspire to be resilient, empathetic, and dignified.

(2)

Given the characteristics of Zhang's poetry, how should I translate it? There have been many approaches to translation. As translation of Chinese poetry into English is concerned, Western translation moved historically from missionaries to sinologists, and then to aesthetes. Their divide in purposes diverges their translation approaches into domesticating the original or foreignizing the translation. Meanwhile, Chinese translators have focused more on translating English poetry into Chinese, and their debate about translation has centered on three criteria—faithfulness, expressiveness, and eloquence.

All these approaches exist for good reasons and work well for one purpose or another. However, I shun the models set up by the foreignizing vs domesticating dichotomy and its implications, as well as the rigid understanding of the Chinese translators' three criteria. I am not ready to sacrifice accuracy for stylistic elegance nor elegance for accuracy because turning a Chinese poem into a poetically cogent English one should be a matter of exercising moderation. It's about creative ways of using language, and sensitivity to audience reception. I agree with Fusheng Wu that "great works of translation, like great works of any art, often cannot be fully 'framed' or accounted for by a general theory. They demand individual treatment, which must be rooted in the specific times and circumstances of their production" (115). Thus, the three hats I wear decide which poems I translate, how I translate, and what appearance I fashion for them. Most importantly, I firmly believe good poetry translation should be good poetry in and of itself.

I illustrate what I mean by discussing the translation of a few poems in this volume.

In “Forms” (形色 See page 191) the title word of the poem could be Forms or Rūpa. Rūpa is a Buddhist term. It includes anything that has impact upon the human senses (which is “real” in Buddhist terms), such as people’s dreams, ideas, memories, thoughts (Ingram and Loy 99, 100, and 103), and in this poem’s case, the flowers and names. The speaker obviously realizes the fluidity, transiency, and ephemeral nature of the self. If Rūpa were chosen as the translation, the poem would be domesticated as it shows a strong urge to channel English readers to read the translation in Buddhist or religious terms, which the poem connotes. When translated as Forms, the “story” dwells in this world but with philosophical or Buddhist subtlety. Zhang is not a Buddhist, but as most Chinese use Buddhist concepts in their lives, I keep the nonreligious dimension of the poem. Moreover, the fact that the speaker is obviously obsessed with having a name, a beautiful name, and a famous name shows that the speaker has not achieved the Buddhist non-self, or the universal “oneness” (Barash 88). Therefore, the word Forms sounds faithful to the original poem, but the Buddhist connection is also well kept.

While the above translation pays attention to denotation and connotation, and differences in understanding Buddhism between Easterners and Westerners, my translation of “The Mushroom Spoke, and the Wood Ear Listened” entails another type of flexibility. There are several choices for 木耳, a mushroom that grows on fallen tree trunks and used in cooking: fungus, edible wood fungus, cloud ear, or tree ear. I chose “wood ear” because it’s perfect for the situation. The two dried fellows are level in the same bathtub, and one spoke and the other obviously needed an ear or ears to listen, especially when the poem uses personification! This choice is neither due to domesticating (Fungus does carry a nasty connotation) nor foreignizing (Wood ear is chosen more because the two fellows need to be in the same bathtub and equal in status than it is an effort to do a literal translation).

While these word choices are in correlation with contextual nuance, "Haystack" (草垛 See page 100) juggles two cultures and revolves around a rock. Here, which word should be chosen for 石头? Rock, stone, pebble? Given the youth and mischievous behavior of the speaker, the warm sentiment the speaker feels now, the varied gender possibilities for "you," the rock seems a more proper choice; it is more substantial than a pebble, and smoother than a stone in denotation. Besides, in Chinese, there is the idiomatic saying "egg hitting a rock" that means "overestimating one's strength or oneself, not knowing one's own limitations." So, using the word rock can readily bring out the allusion and accompanying image of innocence and exclusive relationship. Is this foreignization? Maybe, but it is simply a faithful and felicitous choice.

Other times my choice hinges upon a reflection of language sensibility. For instance, in "The River That Would Never See the Sea" (看不见大海的河流 See page 20), the father of the speaker responds by body language to the speaker's question about the Yanzhi River's destination. The original poem treats the father shaking his head as one reaction and pointing to the sky as another. Two images ensue, which are both used by the speaker to speculate on the metaphysical origin of the river or human life. The poem is about the speculative intellect of the Emersonian man-thinking type of father and son. However, it would be awkward or unnatural to use "reactions" in the lines "I deliberated over his reaction for many years" and "my father's reaction" in English. Therefore, I opted for the singular form, which alters neither the feel nor meaning of the poem at all.

My decisions are often as cultural as they are linguistic. Translation is mediated transmission, thus the site of interaction for beliefs, values, and structures with disparate origins. Choosing a word could be a cultural decision. For example, Zhang had a pet dog, called Hua Dan, and the poet's close relationship with the dog is reflected in many of his poems in this volume. In these poems, Hua Dan is either a personal buddy, a family member, or a sentient philosophical being. Some of the poems are written in the second person narration, which does not generate any complexity for translation, but others are written in the third person. In those cases, to translate means to juggle cultural differences.

For instance, the title of "Remembering My Dog in the Year of the Dog" already indicates the poem's focus, the oxytocin-infused relationship between human beings and their canine friends. Zhang conveys his love for his dog, but does it by saying how much his dog, not himself, had already missed him while the dog was still alive. What pertains to translation is that despite Zhang's close relationship with Hua Dan, he uses the pronoun它/it to refer to his dog. In the West, dog owners would use "he" or "she" to refer to their dog depending on the dog's gender, whereas Chinese dog owners, though they love their dogs dearly, still likely use "it" as it is traditional. So, which pronoun to use? I chose she/her/hers because these pronouns make the translation better attuned to the sense and sensibility of the Western readers, and they align better with the sentiment the poem presents. It turns out domesticating the original can be more faithful to the original. The change of pronouns helps the readers feel closer to what the poet feels.

A unique characteristic of Zhang's poems is that they often use no end of the line punctuation or stanza division. As the volume shows, Zhang's repertoire is minimal—occasional inverted commas, dashes, and periods within the lines. For inverted commas, I sometimes opted for italics. For instance, in "He Who Searches for the Signal" and "The Span," I adopted italics to indicate words spoken by the characters. I could have chosen inverted commas, but because Zhang usually uses no end of the line punctuation marks, I avoided that by choosing italics instead.

Where Zhang manifests a rare degree of confidence in and linguistic awareness of what makes poetry is syntax. He fashions a tightly coiled syntax for each individual poem. Such powerful play of syntax, typographical extension as a condition of syntactical progress, makes the poems almost painting-like in effect, which is particularly enjoyable for most readers. For instance, when reading "Sketch of a Winter Day" (冬日速写 See page 146) the hand of the poet creates a pastoral picture in a few strokes. Though they appear last, the magpies on the twigs are prominent in this image, their black and white contour literally visible and their chirping clear and sweet. Each of the previous lines opens the bucolic vista wider and wider, with the last two lines pushing the poem to the summit of aesthetic beauty. Zhang has written many such picturesque poems, some of which are found in this volume, such as "Three Days After the Snow," "Sunday Snow," "Old Days," and "Spring Equinox."

Distorting syntax in translation reduces and deforms meaning, and the poems can be syntactically vandalized. With stops added, there would be less desirable visual flow and, in some cases, ambiguity and complexity. Therefore, I kept the syntactic layout of Zhang's lines without sacrificing the fluency of the English version. Except for rare situations, translations in this volume adhere to the line arrangements of Zhang's poems. This is usually a challenge to translators as discussed in many translational studies. It comes natural for me as a native speaker of Chinese and a speaker who learned English both from a formal education as well as decades of language immersion. This advantage lends my translations a high degree of faithfulness, fluency and ease. For illustration, while English translations are often longer than their Chinese originals, my translations are generally equal in length by sticking to the original syntax.

In total, 183 poems are selected from Zhang's award-winning collections, *Wild Flowers on the Plateau* and *The Everlasting Pot.* These poems are arranged into groups with quotes from great English poems to showcase how Zhang engages with major elements of poetry writing: definition of poetry, writer's personae, deployment of poetic devices, poetry's depth and heights, poet's family background, varieties of poems (including untitled poems, longer poems with stanza division that are rare in Zhang's writing, and poems in the traditional Chinese farewell poem fashion), and a supply of additional Zhang poems for further exploration. As a college professor, I hope it facilitates fun, but also some versatility for pedagogical use. On a more ambitious note, this volume marks the first book-length English-language edition of Zhang's poetry, providing access to the writings of a major contemporary Chinese poet.

目 录

CONTENTS

篇三　荒野向它涌起，/ 在四周绵延，不再荒野

III. The wilderness rose up to it (the jar), /and sprawled around, no longer wild.

IV. Beauty is truth, truth beauty, — that is all.

篇五 我们怎么能区分舞蹈和跳舞人?

V. How can we know the dancer from the dance?

篇六　燕燕于飞，下上其音

VI. Oh swallows, sing in varied note/to each other for sweet succor.

篇七 一个人本身就是一座城市

VII. A man in himself is a city.

篇一 诗应当不言/而自明

I. *A poem should not mean/ but being.*

万古烧

我买了一口好锅
可以用一辈子的那种
陶土的，有松木盖的
只要天塌不下来
我就可以一直用它
煲汤，烧肉
但更多的时候我宁愿
它就那样闲置着
像我一样空空如也
却不可测度

THE EVERLASTING POT

I bought a good pot
one that can last a whole life
made of clay, with a pinewood lid
As long as the sky does not collapse
I can use it all the time
to cook soup, stew meat
But more often I'd rather
it just lay idle there
like me, empty
yet unfathomable

写诗是……

WRITING POETRY IS …

写诗是干一件你从来没有干过的活
工具是现成的，你以前都见过
写诗是小儿初见棺木，他不知道
这么笨拙的木头有什么用
女孩子们在大榕树下荡秋千
女人们把毛线缠绕在两膝之间
写诗是你一个人爬上跷跷板
那一端坐着一个看不见的大家伙
写诗是囚犯放风的时间到了
天地一窟窿，烈日当头照
写诗是五岁那年我随我哥哥去抓乌龟
他用一根铁钩从泥洞里掏出了一团蛇
我至今还记得我的尖叫声
写诗是记忆里的尖叫和回忆时的心跳

Writing poetry is doing something you have never done before
the tools are off the shelf, and you have seen them all
Writing poetry is seeing a coffin; the child doesn't know
what to make out of the clumsy wood
Girls are swinging under the big banyan tree
and women are winding yarn with their knees
Writing poetry is you mounting onto a seesaw
at the other end of which sits an invisible big fellow
Writing poetry is an inmate being let out to exercise
in the hole between heaven and earth, and in the scorching sun
Writing poetry is me at five catching turtles with my elder brother
who using a metal hook dragged out from a mud hole a twine
of snakes
I still remember my shrill screams
Writing poetry is screaming in memory and heart pounding
in reminiscing

左对齐 LEFT ALIGN

一首诗的右边是一大块空地	To the right of a poem is vast empty space
当你在左边写下第一个字	When you write down the first word on the left
脑海里立刻浮现出一个栽秧的人	the image of a man transplanting rice seedlings comes to the mind
滴水的手指上带着春泥	Water dripping from his mud-coated fingers
他将在后退中前进	he shall march forward as he moves backwards
一首诗的右边像弯曲的田埂	To the right of a poem is the curvy ridge of rice fields
你走在参差不齐的小道上	Walking on the uneven surface
你的脚踩进了你父亲的脚印中	your feet stamp into the footprints of your father
你曾无数次设想过这首诗的结局	You have thought countless times about the poem's end
而每当回到左边	yet whenever you return to the left
总有一种意犹未尽的感觉	you feel you still have not fully expressed yourself
一首诗的左边是一个久未归家的人	To the left of a poem is a man who has left home too long
刚刚回家又要离开的那一刻	The moment he arrives home he's ready to depart again
他一只脚已经迈出了门槛	his one foot is already outside of the threshold
另外一只还在屋内	and his other still inside
那一刻曾在他内心里上演过无数次	That moment he had once rehearsed numerous times

笤帚经过大地的声音

SOUND OF A BROOM SWEEPING ACROSS THE EARTH

笤帚经过大地的声音
被我在这个秋天制造了出来
在这首诗中我看见了你屋后的竹林
你父亲用皲裂的虎口掐回一捆毛毛竹
他插在腰间的篾刀上有三个豁口
他胸前的扣子不知什么时候掉了两颗
他制造的这把笤帚被你带到了秋天
烧荒的烟雾从林中空地升起来
夜风在这首诗中随意吹拂
我制造了一种声音——它
紧贴干硬的混凝土，紧贴着
这秋天里的每一个清晨和黄昏
如果你父亲还活着
此刻他一定在某个角落
用你熟悉又陌生的那双手
紧锁着自己的领口

The sound of a broom sweeping across the earth
has been created by me this fall
In the poem I see a bamboo grove behind your house
where the chapped hands of your father gathered a bundle of
bamboo sticks
Three chips showed up on his bamboo knife
Two buttons missing from the front of his shirt at unknown times
You brought this broom made by him into autumn
In an open area in the forest smoke from burning waste grass rose
into the sky
Night wind blew at will in this poem
I created a sound—it
stays close to hard concrete, close to
each dusk and dawn of this fall
Were your father still alive
at present he would be in a certain corner
his hands familiar and strange to you
covering his collar

在黑暗中写诗

最近多有失眠
身处黑暗像一个靶子
被诗句冷不丁射中
拔箭的时候发现
有的箭矢穿心而去
无影无踪，而有的
根本就没有命中靶心
在黑暗中写诗
每写一句都有如光柱射往虚空
我用过最多五节电池的电筒
我身体里的光已经透支
它们去得最远的地方
也是你最不愿意
让我看见的伤心处

WRITING POETRY IN DARKNESS

Recently I have suffered much from insomnia
Situated in darkness like a target
I was surprised by onslaughts of poetic lines
pulling the arrow only to reveal
some arrows had penetrated through the heart
and went traceless, while others
totally missed the target's center
Writing poetry in darkness
each line like a beam of light towards emptiness
I've used as powerful a flashlight as a 5-cell
exhausting all that's in me
The farthest place the lines have reached
is heartbreaking recess that
you do not want me to access

梦见一首诗

有时候我会梦见一首诗
她在梦中的样子无比清晰
她握我的手像小时候
我用力捏紧铅笔头
笔芯折断了
我鼓足勇气找她借转笔刀
我梦见一首诗在跳房子
而我在一旁摇跳绳
绳子的另一端拴在无皮的枣树干上
我梦见我使劲摇动地上的尘土
像牛犊发了狂，前撅后拱
我看见她闭上眼睛越跳越高
我梦见所有的事物都是发光体
我一转身它们就熄灭
有时候我在一首诗里闪烁
梦醒之后才发现
我从来不曾带走过任何梦中之物

I DREAM OF A POEM

Sometimes I dreamed of a poem
her appearance in my dream incredibly clear
She held my hand as in childhood
I held my pencil head so tightly and hard
that the point broke
and I had to muster the courage to borrow her sharpener
I dreamed of a poem playing hopscotch
while I was turning a rope
its other end tied to the thin trunk of a jujube tree
I dreamed of myself spinning the rope to bring up dust
like a crazy calf, my belly protruding and my back arching
I see her closing her eyes and jumping higher and higher
In my dream all things were glowing
but as soon as I turned my back they dimmed
Sometimes I would glow in a poem
Once waking up I would find
I could never retrieve anything from my dreams

玫瑰与月季

当一个诗人无法说出
诗是什么的时候
玫瑰与月季在一旁竞相开放
当一首诗呼之欲出
诗人的鼻尖上沁出了汗珠
而她的脸颊上泛出了玫瑰红
月季开出了玫瑰的花
玫瑰在一旁默默承受
我爱的女人无一不热爱花朵
而我爱她们趋身花丛时的尖叫
而不深究什么是月季什么是玫瑰
当我终于有了爱的自觉
诗是什么已经不重要了
重要的是我已经学会了如何
将偶然之爱混淆于必然之爱中

ROSE AND CHINESE ROSE

When a poet cannot explain
what poetry is
rose and Chinese rose compete to open up next to one another
When a poem is on the tip of the tongue
the tip of the poet's nose sweats
while rosy color capers on her cheeks
The Chinese rose bears the flowers of the rose
while the rose endures in silence
Each woman I adore without exception loves flowers
while I love to hear her squeals as she falls for the flowers
without being bothered by the differences between the two roses
When I am finally conscious of love
what poetry is no longer matters
What matters is that I've learned
to envelop accidental love into inevitable love

关于我的睡姿

我没有见过我的睡姿
当我像虾米一样
蜷曲，或者像个十字架形
我能感觉到身体正在挣脱
梦中人赋予它的原形
我总是在入睡前翻来覆去
而入睡后难道会像一片云？
我这样设计过
与你同床共枕
的情景——两朵云
如胶似漆叠加在一起
雨在下面，雨一直在下
我一直这样保持着干涸的模样
像你小时候在泥塘里见过的
那条挣扎着的鱼
当它放弃了挣扎
也就完成了命运对它的塑形

ABOUT MY SLEEPING POSITION

I have never seen my sleeping position
When like a shrimp
I curl up, or spread like a cross
I can feel my body breaking free from
the shape the dreamer endowed it
I often toss and turn in bed before falling asleep
Is it possible I act like a cloud during sleep?
I have imagined
sharing a bed with you
like this—two clouds
stick to each other like lacquer
rain underneath falling all along
and I remain dried up the whole time
like what you saw in the pond during childhood
a flopping fish
when it gave up wiggling
fate also shaped it as meant to be

冰箱贴

做菜的间隙
我时常打量
形状各异的
冰箱贴
这些五颜六色的
小东西都是我
从各地搜集来的
代表着世界
大和美
此生我见过人间的一部分
还有余力去更多的地方
所以需要一口好冰箱
储存足够的食物
我需要
用动物的眼睛看待
锅里的和碗里的
再用人类的目光端详
看不穿的生活
那是亲爱的皮囊
制造出来的动静
我将成全我
在明朗的人间
做一个风尘仆仆的人

FRIDGE MAGNETS

During cooking breaks
I often examine
the varied shaped
magnets on my fridge
These colorful
knickknacks
collected by me from different places
represent the world
its size and beauty
I have seen parts of the world
and still have energy to cover more
So I need a good refrigerator
to stock an adequate amount of food
I need to
adopt animals' eyes to deal with
what's in the pot and what's in my bowl
and use human perspective to scrutinize
the inscrutable life
which is my dear body's
own doings
I shall enable myself
to become in this bright world
a weary, way-worn wanderer

据我所知

并无真正摆脱了写的诗
当诗成为必需，写下
就意味着和上帝对掷骰子
我父亲用沉默的一生告诉我
失败并非多么难堪之事
这个终生都不认他父亲的男人
临终之际哀求我
一定要弄清楚他的父亲是谁
据我所知，诗歌无法回答
这么高深莫测的问题
诗歌长在耕耘过的田间地头
在种子埋下去之后
在菜花盛开之前
这段时间充满了不确定性
我乐于在暮春回家
尾随在一个个消逝的背影后面
他们也是掷过骰子的人
输得心平气和
而越是平静，就越能靠近
所谓的诗意，据我所知
写诗的目的就是为了能成为
这样一位不知所踪的父亲

AS FAR AS I KNOW

I am not really detached from my poetry
When poetry becomes a necessity, writing
means throwing dice with God
My father taught me with his whole life
failing is not so embarrassing
This man who never acknowledged his own father
beseeched me at his death bed
to figure out who his father had been
As far as I know, poetry cannot answer
such an unfathomable question
Poetry grows from tilled fields
After seeds are sown
before rapeseed flowers bloom
is a period of uncertainty
I enjoy returning home in late spring
following the back view of many disappeared
They flung dice as well and
they remained calm at their failure
Yet the calmer they were, the closer they were
to what is known as the poetic. As far as I know
the purpose of writing poetry is
to become such an elusive father

被词语找到的人

平静找上门来了
并不叩门，径直走近我
对我说：你很平静
慵懒找上门来了
带着一张灰色的毛毯
挨我坐下，将毛毯一角
轻轻搭在我的膝盖上
健忘找上门来了
推开门的时候光亮中
有一串灰尘扑扑的影子
让我用浑浊的眼睛辨认它们
让我这样反复呢喃：你好啊
慈祥从我递出去的手掌开始
慢慢扩展到了我的眼神和笑容里
我融化在了这个人的体内
仿佛是在看一部默片
大厅里只有胶片的转动声
当镜头转向寂寥的旷野
悲伤找上门来了
幸存者爬过弹坑，铁丝网和水潭
回到被尸体填满的掩体中
没有人见识过他的悔恨
但我曾在凌晨时分咬着被角抽泣
为我们不可避免的命运
为这些曾经以为遥不可及的词语
一个一个找上门来
填满了我
替代了我

FOUND BY WORDS

Peace approached my door
instead of knocking, it walked straight to me
uttering: You look peaceful
Ennui approached my door
with a grey wool blanket
sitting by my side to lay a corner of the blanket
gently onto my knees
Forgetfulness approached me
when it pushed open my door, and in
brightness
a line of dusty shadows
asked me to identify them with my cloudy eyes
and to murmur repeatedly: hi
Kindness spread from my extended palms
slowly to my eyes and smile
I melt inside this human being
as if viewing a silent movie
in a hall where only the turning of the films
was audible
When the camera directed towards the desolate
wilderness
sadness approached my door
The survivor climbed over craters, barbed
wire, and water puddles
to return to the bunker full of dead bodies
No one saw his repentance
but I once chewed the quilt corner and sobbed
at dawn
for our unavoidable destiny
for those previously elusive words that have
one by one
replenished me
and replaced me

到树顶上找风

SEARCHING FOR THE WIND ON TREETOPS

有时候我们需要爬到树顶上	Sometimes we needed to climb to the treetops
去寻找风。有时候	to search for the wind. Other times
我们散布在房前屋后的	we spread out around the house
柳树、槐树、皂角树和苦楝树下	under willows, pagoda trees, honey locusts, and chinaberries
抱紧树身往树上爬	and climbed by holding the trunks tightly
有时候我们需要沿途使劲	Still other times we needed to vehemently
摇晃树枝，大声呼唤着	shake the branches, holler loudly
慢慢从树梢上探出头	and then slowly stick out our head from the treetops
有时候我探出头看见	Sometimes I would poke my head out to see
你的父亲在芝麻地里蠕动	your dad crawling in a sesame field
他的母亲还在河边割猪草	and his mom still cutting grass by the river for pigs
有时候我看见田间里的稻草人	Other times I would see the field's scarecrow
好像换了一件外套	in a new outfit
我们从树上溜下来	and we would slip down the trees
踩着牛背，或牛角	mount onto a buffalo, or hold onto its horn
牛蝇扇动的风只有牛蝇感觉到了	while only the gadflies felt the wind they stirred up
有时候我们就这样爬上爬下	Still other times we would repeatedly climb up and down
耗尽了汗水，目的是	shed all sweat, and let
等雨水来重新把我们滋润	the rain nurture us one more time

高原上的野花

WILD FLOWERS ON THE PLATEAU

我愿意为任何人生养如此众多的小美女
我愿意将我的祖国搬迁到
这里，在这里，我愿意
做一个永不愤世嫉俗的人
像那条来历不明的小溪
我愿意终日涕泪横流，以此表达
我真的愿意
做一个披头散发的老父亲

I'd love to sire for anyone so many little beauties
I'd love to move my homeland
here; and here, I'd love to
be one who is never cynical
like that creek of unknown origins
I'd love to shed grateful tears all day long, to convey
my genuine willingness
to be the old father with billowing hair

篇二 用心，这是我们永远要做的正经事

II. *To pay attention, this is our endless and proper work.*

断流河抒怀

THOUGHTS ON THE DRYING—UP RIVER

每一条河流都有自己的出路
当第一滴暴雨落在荆山之巅
这雨滴就意识到了若干年后
若干年后我站在干涸的河床上
仰望喧嚣的星空，每一滴星光
都那么微弱而倔强，就像我
卑微而倔强地走在这条断流河上
身前身后都是滔滔巨浪
生前生后都有人潮汹涌

Each river ends at the river's mouth
When the first raindrop of a storm fell on the summit of Mt. Jing
it already knew its final place years later
Years later I stand on a dried-up riverbed
Up in the starry sky, I see light
weak yet willful, just like me
humble and headstrong walking on this dried-up river
Before and behind me there were torrential waves
Before and after my life, waves of people

旅游札记

TRAVEL NOTES

我有对床的恐惧
越是宽大整洁的床
这恐惧越盛
冬天即将来临
旷野不再拥挤
我有对旅途中孤零零的客栈的恐惧
怀着不安再看一眼
清凉的落日，和
浸泡在窗外河道里的枯枝
关上门窗
我坐在堆着四只枕头的床上
仿佛坐在地球上最荒凉的地方
这么宽大而整洁的荒凉
像这首诗一样

I am afraid of beds
The more immaculate and bigger the bed is
the more intense my fear
Winter is coming
and the wilderness is no longer crowded
I am afraid of this lonesome inn on my journey
Nervously I take another look
at the cooling sunset, and
dying branches on the riverbed outside the window
With the window closed
I sit among four pillows on my bed
as if sitting in the most desolate place on earth
Such vast and immaculate desolation
feels just like this poem

看不见大海的河流

岩子河永远也不会看见大海
我父亲也没有见过
平日里，河水慵懒
只有在暴雨过后它才激动起来
我问过父亲：河水会流向哪里?
父亲摇摇头，过后又指指天
这两个动作让我想了很多年
多年以后我从海边归来
独自坐在泄洪道口
刚下过暴雨，白浪奔逐
我在轰鸣声中想起了
父亲的那两个动作
摇头时我满脸水雾
抬头见烟雨中的老父亲
正在堤坝上使劲地朝我挥手

THE RIVER THAT WOULD NEVER SEE THE SEA

The Yanzhi River would never see the sea
neither would my father
Oftentimes, the river was lackadaisical
getting excited only after a storm
I once asked my father: Where will it reach?
He shook his head, and then pointed to the sky
I deliberated over his reaction for many years
Years later I returned from the sea
As I sat alone at the floodgates of the spillway
waves were chasing one another after the storm
In their crashing sounds I recalled
my father's reaction
When he shook his head I was clueless
When I lifted my head in misty rain I saw him
waving hard to me from the riverbank

# 一点生活	# A PINCH OF LIFE
超市总把盐袋放在角落	The grocery store always tucks away the salt in a corner
那地方你一年也光顾不了几次	which you frequent no more than a few times a year
而在自家的厨房里	while in your own kitchen
盐罐被摆放在显眼的位置	the salt jar is always placed in a prominent position
一只青花瓷瓶已经有些年份	The blue and white porcelain jar has seen better years
瓶盖并非原配	covered by a lid that's not the original
你站在灶台边，往滚烫的油锅内	You stand by the cooktop, throwing into the pan of boiling oil
扔一些冷冰冰的东西	some cold ingredients
你喜欢听它们的嗞嗞声	You love the sizzling sounds
这声音唤醒了很多年前的	that awakes memory of years past
某个午时，黄昏	a certain afternoon, near dusk
你趴在灶沿看母亲	you watched from the cooking area your mother
在烟雾中挥舞锅铲	wielding a spatula in the smoke
来回翻炒着寡淡的锅底	and stirring this way and that the dull bottom of a pot
从那时起你就相信	Since then you've believed
津津有味的生活源于这	palatable life originates from
一丝丝清晰的记忆	traces of clear memories

芡实与菱角

FOX NUTS AND BAT NUTS

巨大的木盆漂浮
在更为巨大的水面上
年幼的我坐在水盆中央
这是我第一次离开陆地
前往芡实和菱角的家乡
巨大的秋阳照耀着平静的水面
我在明晃晃的年纪里就有了
湿漉漉的记忆，这记忆
通往芡实和菱角的家乡
大人们关心水下有什么
而我只对水面上的事物感兴趣
用力划动的木盆左摇右晃
我要去我从没去过的地方
我要采摘那些水中的果实
把它们运回陆地
把它们的家乡运回我的家乡

The large wood bucket floated
on the even larger water surface
me the little boy sitting in the bucket center
It was my first sailing away from the land
to the home of fox nuts and bat nuts
The large autumn sun shone on the placid water
and I gained at a glowing age
wet memories, memories leading to
the hometown of fox nuts and bat nuts
The adults were interested in what's beneath the water
while I was only keen on what's above
Rowing and rocking the bucket left and right
I shall travel to places I had never been
I shall harvest the fruits of water
I shall transport them to the land
I shall move their hometown to mine

反刍的人

埋在米糠里的鸡蛋
封在坛子里的猪油
挂在屋梁上的腊肉
晾在簸箕上的薯干
摊在筛子里的腌鱼
倒扣在腌菜坛中的辣椒
堆放在火塘角落的花生
藏在竹林地窖里的红薯
悬在树丫上的丝瓜和葫芦
沉睡在草丛中的老南瓜
——哦，十根指头
已经不够用了
第十一根是香烟
供你在饭后反刍
第十二根是铁钉
好多年前就被钉在了墙上
好多年前它就已经生锈了
当它什么都不挂的时候
它连锈迹也挂不住

THE ONE WHO RUMINATES

Eggs buried in rice bran
Lard sealed in a jar
Bacon hanging from the roof beam
Sliced potatoes drying in a winnowing fan
Salted fish lying in a traditional sieve
Peppers pressed upside down in the pickling crock
Peanuts piled in a corner near the firepit
Sweet potatoes stored away in a cellar in the bamboo forest
Luffas and gourds dangling from tree branches
Old pumpkins slumbering in the grass
— Oh, ten fingers
are already not enough for counting
The eleventh is for cigarettes
to accompany your rumination
The twelfth is a nail
driven into the wall many years ago
rusting since years ago
When it holds nothing
it can hardly support the rust

到梦里去

TO ENTER YOUR DREAM

直到昨晚我才发现
所谓睡眠
不过是牧羊人
在天黑之前把四散在天边的
羊群赶进栅栏
每一只羊都有
一个月明星稀的夜晚
每一位牧羊人身边
都有一堆干牛粪
昨天晚上我发现
我仍是脱缰之马可供你消遣
到梦里去
到梦里去
我的羊群慢慢聚拢
背靠背在黑暗中
挤成一团
而你在月光下甩打响鞭
每抖一下手腕
我就往你胸前靠近一点

I did not realize until last night
the so-called sleep
is nothing but the shepherd
before dark gathering his widely scattered
flock into the pen
Each sheep gets
a moonlit night
Each shepherd has by his side
a pile of dry cow dung
Last night I realized
I am still that wild horse for you to rein
in your dream
To enter your dream
my flock is gradually gathering
and back-to-back in darkness
huddling
When you crack your whip in moonlight
each move of your wrist
brings me closer to your chest

翠鸟的一天	A DAY OF THE KINGFISHER
河面上有一层白雾	The Yanzhi River wears a white veil of fog
太阳光顾岩子河半晌了	The sun has shown above the river for a while
还没有散开	but has not spread its light
翠鸟站在河沿边光秃秃的野枣枝上	The kingfisher stands by the river on a wild jujube's bare branch
像一颗意外的野枣	like an accidental jujube date
随时准备弹向更意外的地方	ready to catapult to a more accidental place
从前的小河流着流着	The erstwhile stream flowed and flowed
变成了一座水库	and has turned into a reservoir
那些清粼粼的时光仿佛不曾有过一样	as if all those clear and crystalline days had not existed
但翠鸟能证明这世上并不存在幻象	Yet the kingfisher proves there were no illusions
它贴近水面一遍遍疾飞	It takes repeated flights, fast and close to the water's surface
就像当年站在岸边打水漂的少年	just like the young man once did, skimming stones on the bank
从早到晚都在努力	from morning till night without giving up
将一片片石头送过	sending stone after stone across
越来越宽阔的河面	the ever-widening river

雨没有下透　THE RAIN ABATED TOO SOON

牛尾在午后的田埂上来回甩动	On the afternoon field ridges buffalo tails sway to and fro
这自我鞭策的活物	Such self-motivated creatures
总有一天会走远走出我的生活	one day will surely walk far away and out of my life
但在此之前，泥泞依然	But before that, it's still muddy
天地严丝合缝	and heaven and earth leave no opening for getaway
从牛背上溜下来的人	He who slides down from the back of a buffalo
被牛蝇惹恼了，抓起荆条	annoyed by gnats, grabs twigs of chaste trees
来回抽打自己的后背和前胸	and beats repeatedly his front and back
这自我鞭策的活物	Such a self-motivated creature
总有一天会来到我的眼前	one day will surely appear before me
在这首郁闷的诗中与我	in this depressing poem
相恨，相逢	to regret meeting late

找信号的人

HE WHO SEARCHES FOR THE SIGNAL

我的朋友魏天无给我讲过
一个故事，故事的主人公
生活在祁连山深处
那天他要通过 QQ 视频参加
农村生源自主招生面试
到了约定的时间
却没有出现在视频中
事后考官们才知道他没有电脑
他当时正翻山越岭寻找手机信号
我无数次想象过这样的
镜头：一个青年举着手机
奔跑在山岗上
山顶摇晃，永远不够高
他一边跑一边对着镜头大呼小叫
再也没有更高的山了
再也没有比先前诅咒过
如今还需要再诅咒一遍的生活
更让人无可奈何的了
我曾无数次陷在这样的生活中
张开嘴巴，却一言不发

My friend Wei Tianwu once told me
a story, the protagonist of which
lived deep in the Qilian Mountains
That day the young man was scheduled for a video interview
for independent enrollment of students from rural areas
But by the interview time
he did not show up
Later the examiners learned he lacked a computer
and was looking for phone signals all over the mountaintop
I have replayed in my mind many times
such a scenario: a young man holding a cell phone
runs on a mountaintop
The mountaintop wobbles, never high enough for any signals
While running the young man shouts to the phone
No higher spots
This fucking
and today fucked up again life
Nothing sucks more than this
I had been trapped countless times in such a life
mouth wide open yet silent

一只蚂蚁出门了 AN ANT VENTURED OUT

一只蚂蚁出门了	An ant ventured out
早上我在小花园门口看见它	In the morning I saw it at the gate of the small garden
晚上我在石拱桥头看见它	At dusk I came across it near one end of the bridge
一只蚂蚁有好运气	The ant was lucky
我祝它明天也像今天	I wish tomorrow, as today, it can also
能够翻过一具具尸体	crawl over corpse after corpse
还能背着多余的	and even bring extra
尸体回家	corpses home

在涠洲岛看落日

SUNSET VIEW ON WEIZHOU ISLAND

我在涠洲岛上看见了最纯粹的落日
我在日落大海之际看见了
最真实的我，可以对视的
那个我，接受了孤独和黑暗的我
圆满的一天将终结于此
幸福的人在沙滩上像孩子
来回寻找被潮汐带上岸的杂什
幸福的沙子随波逐流
却没有卑微之感
我在一年将尽之时走到了自己的身旁
我挨我坐下就像终于挨着了你
手指轻拍膝盖
身体里有呼啸声应和着
闪烁的波浪，动荡的太平洋
我知道，这是我仍有把握
以诗之身活在人间的真正原因

I saw the purest sunset on Weizhou Island
I saw at the moment the sun touched the sea
my truest self, the one that could stand
gaze, the one that absorbed loneliness and darkness
A perfect day was drawing to its end
Happy people like children on the beach
sought back and forth what tidal waves brought onshore
Happy sand drifted along with the flow
without feeling insignificant
I approached myself in the very last moment of the year
I sat down, side by side with myself, as if with you
a finger gently tapping on the kneecap
inside me a roaring sound resonating with
the glistening waves, the turbulent Pacific Ocean
I knew, with certainty, why
my body could still live in this world as a poet

抓一把硬币逛菜市

GO TO THE FOOD MARKET WITH A HANDFUL OF COINS

每当活不下去的时候
我会立即起身
从鞋柜上的钱罐里
抓起一把硬币
去菜市场闲逛
每当我叮当作响
走在人群中，内心里
有一种无法抑制的快乐在涌动
这快乐近似于我小时候
摇晃着积攒的钱罐
站在榆钱树下等候货郎的身影
我在五颜六色的菜市摊旁
一遍又一遍走着
当硬币花光时
某种一名不文的满足感
让我看上去不是一般的幸福

When I feel unable to live anymore
I rise like a shot
from the piggy bank on the shoe cabinet
grab a handful of coins
and take a stroll through the food market
When the coins jingle
as I walk among the crowds, my heart
feels the surge of uncontrollable joy
It resembles what I felt when as a little boy
I shook my piggy bank
waiting under an elm tree for the itinerant vendor
I saunter among the colorful food stands
round and round
When the coins are gone
a certain sense of penniless satisfaction
makes me look unusually happy

篇三 荒野向它涌起，/在四周绵延，不再荒野

III. *The wilderness rose up to it (the jar), /and sprawled around, no longer wild.*

腌鱼在滴水

WATER-DRIPPING SALTED FISH

腌鱼在滴水
在白色的冒着热气的阳光下
一排腌鱼都在滴水
水滴由快到慢
由清到浊
最后一滴从鱼眼深处滑下
经由鱼鳍，到达鱼尾
凝聚了一条鱼
最后一点力气
此时落日已被大地吸纳
晚风拉扯着
一旁跳荡的晾衣绳
绳子上挂着粘满了鱼鳞的棉衣
棉衣开始很重，后来很轻

The salted fish are dripping water
Under the heat of the white sunshine
all the fish on the line are dripping
Water fell from fast to slow
clear to cloudy
The last drop slipped down from the depth of the eye
traveling through the fins to the tail
holding
the last ounce of the fish's vigor
By then the ground already absorbed the sunset
Evening wind plucked at
the swaying washing line
on which hung cotton padded coats stained by fish fins
The coats were first heavy and then light

墙边草

墙边草活在它去年死去的地方
和去年一样，那几缕绿
和去年一样，我蹲下来
查看墙缝，又站起来往前走
墙边草原地踏步
在光秃秃的角落强颜欢笑
和去年一样
它不会长得太高
也不会长得太久
如果太辛苦，它就去死
等来生再试试

GRASS AGAINST THE WALL

Grass grows against the wall where it died last year
like those of last year, a few wisps of green,
Like I did last year, I squat down
to check the wall cracks, then move forward
Grass against the wall goes nowhere
in the empty corner it forces a happy smile
Like last year
it can neither grow very tall
nor survive for long
If it is too hard, it gives in to death
till given another try in the next life

今年的最后一首诗

END OF THE YEAR POEM

清理鞋柜的时候发现
大多数鞋子已经不合脚了
你甚至记不起什么时候穿过它
更想不起穿它去过哪里
道路迷失在鞋底
鞋帮已经扭曲
有的甚至左右难分
你把它们逐一拿出来
摆放在门口仿佛看见
家里涌进来了一群人
而此时屋子里异常安静
你赤脚走动时
能听见心脏的扑腾声

While sorting out the shoe cabinet you discover
most shoes no longer fit your feet
You can't even recall when you wore them
nor where you have been in them
Under the shoes your way got lost
The shoe uppers are misshapen
some even hard to tell the left from the right
One by one you take the shoes out
put them at the front door, and seem to see
a crowd thronging into your place
and yet the room is unusually quiet
When walking barefoot
you can hear the thumping of your heart

蟑螂想不明白

COCKROACHES CANNOT UNDERSTAND

蟑螂想不明白为什么
它一出现人人就会喊打
蟑螂在黑暗中
自如爬行，穿梭
每当灯亮的刹那间
它都不知所措
光明填满了黑锅
蟑螂沿着锅沿跑了一圈又一圈
却无法进入黑暗的内部
它要的黑暗远比人类能给予的
辽阔得多

Cockroaches cannot understand why
as soon as they appear everybody wants to kill them
In darkness they
crawl at ease, weaving in and out
As soon as the light is on
they are scared out of their wits
Light fills up the dark wok
scurrying about the wok's brim again and again
the cockroaches cannot pentrate darkness itself
They want from the human world darkness
too vast to give

原来是这样 SO THAT'S HOW IT'S GOT TO BE

我见过竹林里的刺猬	I saw a hedgehog in the bamboo forest
在松软的竹叶上轻巧地爬行	crawling effortlessly on soft bamboo leaves
我见我手持一根竹棍	I saw myself holding a bamboo stick
飞奔过去	galloping towards it
刺猬就地缩成一团	The hedgehog balled up on the spot
我就地蹲下	I squatted down
无计可施	at a loss as to what to do
竹梢上的鸟鸣	Birds chirped on bamboo shoots
竹林里斑驳的日影	The shadow of the sun dappled the forest
我见我从有趣变得无趣	I saw myself change from being interesting to boring
像刺猬一样藏在刺猬中	like a hedgehog among its own kind

红糖与油条

BROWN SUGAR AND YOUTIAO

再过一座松林就到外婆家了
再往前走一段路就能看见
堰塘，菜地和一树梨花
再坚持一会儿夕阳就落山了
湿透的衣服就能被风晾干
好像从来没有怕过鬼
再小跑几步就会听见狗叫
一条花狗堵在三岔路口
再让它嗅一嗅五岁的你吧
你身上有红糖和油条的气味
再让这气味在遥远的年代
多飘荡一会儿

Another pine grove you will reach grandma's house
Another short walk you will see
a pond, vegetable fields, and pear flowers on a tree
Another while the sun will set
and your soaked clothes will be air-dried
as if you had never been afraid of ghosts
Another little trot you will hear barking
from a mottled dog blocking the way at the ford
Let it sniff again the five-year-old you
who smelt of brown sugar and youtiao
Let this scent in the far away time
drift a bit longer

南瓜诗

把一只南瓜分成三等分
两等分送人
剩下的
分三顿吃——
清炒一盘（加辣子）
清蒸一碗（加冰糖）
剩下的做成南瓜饼
我并不想吃南瓜饼
也没有做过南瓜饼
但这只南瓜
来自三百公里外的老家
这么长的藤
只结了这样一只瓜

SONG OF THE PUMPKIN

One pumpkin divided into three portions
Two given away as gifts
The last
cooked for three meals—
stir-fried (added pepper)
steamed (added rock sugar)
the rest fried into pumpkin cakes
I didn't really like to eat pumpkin cakes
nor had I ever made any
But this pumpkin
originated from my family three hundred kilometers away
Such a long vine
yielded only one such pumpkin

迎春花

WINTER JASMINE

迎春花蹲在水边
看着自己的长头发
她感觉自己是别在别人头发上的
一束花
小夫妻带着小儿来踏青
好看的婚姻吸引了湖畔的爱情
小男孩把童子尿撒进花蕊
好听的声音刺激着
他们的爱情

Winter jasmine squatted by water
examining her long hair
She felt herself pinned to another person's hair
like a bouquet
A young couple brought their little son for an outing
their sweet marriage allured lovers by the lake
When the little boy peed into the pistil of a flower
the tinkling sounds stimulated
love between the lovers

秋葵

秋葵怎么做都好吃
怎么念都好听
我记得第一次带你吃它的情形
那是一个夏天
我俩坐在楚灶王的窗边
我一边翻着菜谱一边指着秋葵
说：这个好吃！
我记得你自始至终
一副心满意足的样子
那也是我第一次吃秋葵
第一次觉得我们不在一起
多可惜

OKRA

Okra tastes great however you cook it
It sounds great however you say it
I remember introducing it to you
That was a summer
at Chu Zao Wang restaurant we sat near the window
As I perused the menu, I pointed to okra and
said: This tastes great!
I still recall you appeared throughout the time
to be very content
That was also my first time eating okra
The first time I felt not sharing life with you
would be a great pity

把手伸进别人的兜里

把手伸进别人的兜里
那是什么感觉
如果是一只空兜
正好填满你的手
把手伸进你爱的人的兜里
再也不想拔出来
那是什么感觉
再也不想像今天这样
在冷雨中
在自己的兜里寻找你的手了

PUTTING YOUR HAND IN SOMEONE'S POCKET

Putting your hand in someone's pocket
is what kind of a feeling
If it is an empty pocket
it fits your hand perfectly
Putting your hand in the pocket of whom you love
and never wanting to take it out
is what kind of a feeling
I no longer want it to be like today
in cold rain
searching for your hand in my own pocket

树枝不会因为果实而折断

BRANCHES WON'T BREAK DESPITE THE FRUIT

我们在树下讨论生活的意义
头顶上是密密麻麻的桃子
“比树叶还多。” 有人说
反对的人起身绕着树干来回数
老父亲在一旁偶尔插几句嘴
奇怪的是，每当他话音刚落
就会有一枚桃子落在地上
而更多的桃子还在长
而树枝也将越垂越低
没有人在意不说话的时候
老父亲心里装着什么

We were discussing the meaning of life under the tree
peaches densely packed overhead
"More peaches than leaves," one said
and the opponents rose to walk around the trunk and count
My old father occasionally chimed in
How strange, whenever he finished speaking
a peach would fall onto the ground
and more would grow
and the branches would bend lower and lower
Nobody cared when not speaking
what was in the mind of my old father

何以见得

被春风吹落的树叶含有
那么多的不舍。何以见得?
被春风拉扯着踉跄
在文明路上
都司湖边
何以见得欣悦与悲伤
花圈店里同时在售
纸绢花和
避孕套
阳光照在玻璃柜台上
灯泡在阴冷的室内摇晃
何以见得
生与死不在同一方向

HOW DO WE KNOW THAT

Leaves blown from trees by spring breeze look
so unwilling. How do we know that?
Dragged by spring breeze to dodder
down Wenming Road
along Dusi Lake
how do we know it is joy or sorrow
The florist is selling both
paper flowers
and condoms
while sunlight falls on the glass countertop
and light bulbs shake in the cold room
How do we know
life and death are not heading in the same direction

有些悲哀你不能克服 SOME SADNESS YOU CAN NEVER GET OVER

暴雨把蚯蚓冲出了泥土
无助地蠕动在地表
太阳暴晒的鱼塘里花鲢浮在水面上
你无法帮它们呼吸
被蚊子咬过脖颈的甲鱼半夜死了
发臭的空气中桐花自落
一个人记得回家的路却回不了家
雾霾如衣，穿上了就脱不下来
我看见了你永远看不清你
我看见我消逝在了
你渐渐变冷的心肠中

The storm washed out of the soil the earthworms
that squirmed helplessly on the ground
The silver carp floated on the pond water due to sun
exposure
but you could not help them breathe
The turtle died during midnight from mosquito bites
on the neck
Tung blossoms fell on their own in the putrid air
A person may remember the road home but could
not get back
The smog wore like clothes, once on, hard to take off
I saw you but could never see you clearly
I saw myself vanishing
in your gradually hardening heart

锦鲤

KOI FISH

一条锦鲤游动的时候
池水波澜不兴
两条锦鲤咬着尾巴游
水池呈现出阴阳两极
现在是一池的锦鲤
拥挤着
从此岸涌向彼岸
又从彼岸游了回来
花花绿绿的生活令人眩目
鱼吻轻柔
鱼吻绝望
水花溅得越高的地方
悲伤越集中

When a koi fish swims
pond water remains unfazed
When two koi fish swim closely one after the other
the yin and yang of the pond appear—
With a pond full of koi fish
thronging and swimming
from one end of the pond to the other
then back again to the beginning
against a dizzying backdrop of colorful life
fish kiss tenderly
fish kiss in despair
The higher the place where the waves splash
the denser the sadness

蘑菇说，木耳听

一朵蘑菇与一只木耳共一个浴盆
两个干货飘在水面上
相互瞧不起对方
这样黑，这样干瘪
就这样对峙了一夜
天亮后，两个胖子挤在水里
蘑菇说：“酱紫，酱紫……”
木耳听见了，但木耳不回答
蘑菇与木耳都想回神农架

THE MUSHROOM SPOKE, AND THE WOOD EAR LISTENED

A mushroom and a wood ear shared a bathtub
two dried fellows floating on water
and having no regard for each other
So dark, so dried up
their face-off lasted a night
At daybreak, two fat guys soaked tight in water
The mushroom said: “Hey, hey…”
The wood ear heard but did not respond
Both longed to be back on Shennongjia

白芝麻，黑芝麻

WHITE SESAME, BLACK SESAME

白芝麻比黑芝麻香
黑芝麻比白芝麻有营养
当你把它们拌在一起时
为什么我总是想
把黑芝麻从白芝麻里挑出来
把白芝麻从黑芝麻中捡出去

White sesame is more delicious than black sesame
Black sesame is more nutritious than white sesame
When you blend the two together
why do I always have the urge
to separate the black ones from the white ones
or the white ones from the black ones

日落之后

AFTER SUNSET

日落之后还有很长一段路要走
父亲坐在台阶上
背着慢慢变幻的光
他已经戒烟了，现在又戒了酒
再也没有令他激动的事物
落入池塘的草木填满了池塘
落入鱼篓的鱼安静了认命了
风走在公路上，这是晚风
追着一张纸在跑
路过的少年将捡到
另外一个少年的故事
关于贫穷、成长，关于孤独
再也没有忍受不了的生活
如果我也能够像他这样
在黑暗中独自活到天亮

After sunset there is still a long way to go
My father sits on the steps
against the gradually changing light
He first quit smoking, and now drinking
Nothing can excite him anymore
Fallen grass has filled up the pond
Fish trapped in the basket are quiet, reconciled to fate
Wind is blowing on the road; it's sunset wind
chasing a piece of paper into flight
and a young man passing by will pick up that paper
of another young man's story of
poverty, growth, and loneliness
Life would no longer be unbearable
if I could live like my father
alone in the dark till daylight

唯愿

唯愿我的泡菜坛清亮如初
豆角、竹笋、萝卜和白菜
合乎你的胃口，唯愿
你的味觉还保持着
纯正的天经地义的味觉
红的是辣椒
黄的是姜片
白的是蒜头
你是你，我依然是我
唯愿世道风平浪静
坛沿水永不干枯
我在密封中慢慢发酵
唯愿你来的那天我正好启封
空气中弥漫着你久违的味道

I'D RATHER

I'd like to keep brine in my pickling crock pristine
beans, bamboo shoots, radishes, and cabbages
to your taste; I'd like
you still keep
your natural gustatory sharpness
peppers red
ginger yellow
garlic white
you are you and I, myself
I'd like a calm world
the water in the moat of my crock never dries up
and I ferment slowly in a sealed state
I'd like you to arrive when the lid is opened
and the air permeates with long-lost taste

一团迷雾

A FOG

朋友发来大雾图
他不知道我尚在雾中
很多年了
我们只有面对面的能见度
甚至当我面对
那张挂满凝霜的脸
竟一次次误以为那不是我
不是那个踩着覆满小路的松针
在迷雾里打转的人
太阳在雾外冷眼旁观
那是我见过的
最红的太阳
烙铁一样不可描述

A friend sent me the weather map for fog
not knowing that I was right in a fog
For years
Our visibility was limited to a face-to-face nod
In front of
that frost-covered face
I even repeatedly thought it was not me
that treaded on a pinecone strewn path
and trapped in a fog
Outside the fog the sun looked on unconcerned
It's what I have seen as
the reddest sun
an indescribable iron

河流拐弯的地方

WHERE THE RIVER BENDS

河流拐弯的地方
河水你推我搡
从犹豫，慌乱，到咆哮
直至被彻底驯服
在下一个弯道来临前
当你站在高处平静地眺望
这段无比熟悉的河道
你是否有过不羁的冲动
有好多次
我守候在日落的地方
等着一个人
头破血流地朝我奔过来

Where the river bends
the waters push one another
hesitating, panicking, roaring
until totally tamed
before the next river bend appears
When you look down from a high position
at this very familiar watercourse
have you ever experienced any uncontrollable urge
For many times
I have waited at the sunset place
for a person
to run towards me badly battered

船桨划水的声音

SOUND OF OARS ROWING IN WATER

我住在一座孤岛上
周围都是孤岛
鸟群只在早晚出没
我留意过鸦群起飞时
岛身有一阵晃动
捕鱼船像榛树叶
漂在水面上，其中一片
每天准时飘到我身边
我住在这片树叶上就像
河水住在纵横交织的河道中
我听见划水的声音
每天由早晨的清亮转为
傍晚过后的清凉

I live on a lone island
surrounded by more of its kind
Birds appear only in mornings and evenings
I notice when ravens take flight
the island rocks
Fishing boats like hazel leaves
float on the water's surface, one of which
floats to my side regularly
I live on this leaf just like
water does in the crisscross of rivers
I hear the sound of oars rowing, turning
from clear in the morning to
chilly in the evening

传送带

在场传送带前等候行李的人
应该是这世上最深情的人
耐心，专注，从一而终
在缓缓抵达的各式行李中
没有任何廉价和多余
我在焦虑中看见了
越来越强烈的占有欲
那是最好的自己
带着最美好的感情守望
在遥遥无期的人生之旅
就像真的有一种爱叫望穿秋水
真有这样的爱人
在人世间值得我将自己
从麻木与昏眩中唤醒

CONVEYOR BELT

Those who wait at the airport carousel for their luggage
must be the most loving people in the world
patient, focused, and committed
Varied luggage arriving slowly
they include nothing cheap nor inessential
In anxiety I saw
a stronger and stronger desire to possess
what is the best self
watching for the best emotional attachment
on this endless life journey
as if there were indeed a love that wouldn't disappoint
or indeed such a lover
for whom it is worth trying in this world
to awaken myself from indifference and dizziness

滚铁环

我滚过的最大的铁环
是一只永久牌自行车的轮圈
我用弯钩推着它
摇摇晃晃地上路
八月的星空
高高的谷堆
我绕着晒谷场一边跑
一边想象着黑暗的尽头
当我越跑越快
铁环溅出了火花
我感觉自己已将黑暗推开
而身处黑暗中的父母
放下蒲扇
紧张地望着我
看见我消逝在了黑暗深处

HOOP ROLLING

The biggest hoop I've played with
was the rim of a Forever bike
I guided it with a metal hook
rolling unsteadily down the road
Under the starlit August sky
haystacks of rice straw stood high
While running on the threshing floor
I imagined seeing the end of darkness
As I ran faster and faster
sparks splashed from the hoop
I thought I had pushed away darkness
yet in darkness my parents had
put away their cattail leaf fan
and were nervously watching as I
disappeared into the abyss of darkness

瓢泼

DOWNPOUR

晨起给菜地浇水的人
并不知道傍晚会下雨
他在晨光中来回走
木桶晃荡，葫芦瓢磕磕碰碰
辣椒已经醒了一半
扁豆还睡眼惺忪
我在菜地边看那些泼出去的水
浇地的人手腕抖动，水花轻柔
朝霞很快就要散了
没有云的天空飞过一些叫不上名字的鸟
一天之中我曾有很多次机会
像它们一样隐姓埋名
但总是过于强调自己的感受
直到一场突如其来的暴雨降临
洗刷了这一天的重负
浇地的人回到菜园
两只水桶沮丧地歪倒在角落
葫芦瓢倒扣在地
我感到体内尚有无法排解的热气
顺着眼前的这些藤蔓在袅绕

He who got up early to water the vegetable garden
did not know an evening rain was on the way
He walked about in the morning light
his wooden buckets shaking, gourds knocking against
the rims
Peppers were half awake
and beans, still sleepy
Standing by, I watched as water swung out
gently, from his shaking wrist
Soon morning glow faded
and a few unknown birds flew across the cloudless sky
During each day I had many chances
to stay unknown like the birds did
but I always overemphasized my own feelings
till one sudden rainstorm came
and washed away a whole day's burden
He who had watered the garden returned
his two buckets sitting awry and dejected in a corner
and his gourd lying upside down on the ground
I felt some heat still trapped in my body
winding up along the vines in front of me

鸡冠颂

我喜欢看血红的鸡冠
锯齿一样长在公鸡的头顶
夕阳西下的时候
透过它就能看见
冬日里
雪地上
鸡群零散的爪痕
一只公鸡来回走在爪痕之上
拍打翅膀，警觉地
张望着
踢毽子的我们
河对岸的人也与我们一样
在忙腊月的事情
河对岸的公鸡打鸣了
这是庄严的时刻——
所有的鸡都往鸡笼附近归拢
唯有公鸡独自站在夜幕中
对着河水流逝的方向
鸣叫起来
我在公鸡的叫唤声中
进屋，拉上门闩
在火塘边坐下
周围都是黑夜
我喜欢那个坐立不安的人
墙壁上有他的身影
雪地上有他身体的凹痕

ODE TO COCKSCOMB

I love to see the blood-red cockscomb
growing like a saw on the head of a rooster
As the sun goes down
through the cockscomb I can see
in winter
on snow-covered ground
claw marks scattered here and there
One rooster walked back and forth on the
    claw marks
flapping his wings, vigilantly
watching
us as we children kicked shuttlecocks
Like us residents across the river were
busy with end-of-the-year business
Their rooster crowed
signaling a solemn moment—
All chickens flocked towards the coop
only the rooster stayed behind alone in the
    darkness
Towards the direction where the river flowed
he crowed
To his accompaniment I
entered the house, latched the door
and sat by the fire
with darkness all around
I love the watchful man
on the wall whose shadow flickered
on the snow-covered ground whose body left
    an impression

又见地平线

梦见脚踏车的链子
在追赶你的路上掉了
它早不掉晚不掉
在我刚刚要追上你的时候掉了
空转的轮轴
发出世上最难过的
声音，这声音
仿佛你渐渐远去的背影
被地平线上的风拉扯成了
一缕缕呻吟

SEEING THE HORIZON AGAIN

In my dream the bicycle chain
came off on my way to catch up with you
neither before nor after
but exactly when I was about to reach you
The empty axle
groaned in the saddest
tone, sounding
like your vanishing back
was torn by the wind on the horizon
into a chain of moans

篇四 美即是真，真即是美

IV. *Beauty is truth, truth beauty, —that is all.*

树下听雨

LISTENING TO RAIN UNDER THE TREE

小叶榕有四万七千片叶子
上帝数过
上帝还数过
七亿四千万滴雨水
上帝热爱打击乐
上帝
我在树下
我被蒙在鼓里

The banyan tree has forty-seven thousand leaves
God counted it
God also counted
seven hundred forty million raindrops
God loves percussion music
God
I am under the tree
I am kept in the dark

吹气球

在气球爆炸之前
你不能确定它能被吹多大
在气球爆炸以后
你也不知道它究竟被吹了多大
你一边吹一边抚摸
这个渴望触抚你脸颊的膨胀物
起初它像什么
后来它像什么
在气球爆炸前后
一只气球就这样在想象中膨胀着
你不能确定最后一口气
将在何时终止，你不能确定
一个人由满面通红到一脸茫然
这中间都经历过什么

BLOWING UP A BALLOON

Before a balloon pops
you are not sure how big it can become
After a balloon pops
you are not sure how big it actually became either
You blow and caress
this dilatant that longs to touch your cheeks
What it is like
what it will be like
right before the popping
you are wondering as the balloon expands
You are not sure when the last blowing
will come to an end; and you are not sure
between being red-faced and being dazed
what a person has gone through

七叶一枝花

PARIS POLYPHYLLA, AKA SEVEN-LEAVES-ONE-FLOWER

如果没有“度娘”
我至今还不清楚
七叶一枝花是什么花
如果你没有在电话里提起它
我也已经忘记了
它曾经是一种频繁出没
在我童年里的
花——
那是花吗
一根矮枝
七片叶子
我们翻破山坡上的荆棘
被蜈蚣咬过
也被蛇追着跑
只因为赤脚医生说
它是一味包治百病的药

Had it not been for Baidu the search engine
I would not have been able to know
what kind of flower the Paris plant is
Had you not mentioned it on the phone
I would have totally forgotten
its frequent presence
in my childhood
flowers—
Is it really a flower at all
a short stem
seven leaves
We had bushwhacked for it through thorns on slopes
bit by centipedes
chased by snakes
merely because the barefoot doctor said
it's a cure-all

花饭 FRIED RICE

一碗花饭有若干种吃法	There are many ways to eat a bowl of fried rice
我选择最古老的那种——	I choose the most ancient one —
端着碗，赤脚蹲在多依河边	Holding the bowl, squatting barefoot by the Duoyi River
自己吃一口	one spoon for me
喂鱼儿一口	another for the fish
到最后，碗底现出了彩虹	Finally, on the bottom of my bowl appears a rainbow
我选择用这种目瞪口呆的模样	I choose to use my dumbfounded appearance
来称颂艳丽而呆萌的乳茄	to praise the bright-colored, silly-looking yet adorable nipple fruit
鸟雀在对岸的树梢上	Birds perching on treetops across the river
换着花样叫唤	sing in varied notes
打渔的人撒下网	the fishermen cast a net
并不急于收网	but are in no hurry to draw it in
春天来了，吃饱了饭的人民	Upon the arrival of spring, the well-fed folks
心满意足之余	happy and content
也会像我一样	like I do
在房前屋后乱窜	would then scurry around the house
把每一次散步当成了旅游	taking each walk as a trip

哞哞

MOO-MOO

在汨罗
蓝蓝问我
会不会学牛叫
她话音刚落
就见一头牛
从我胸腔里奔出来
这是一头不会叫的牛
也许它曾经叫过
也许它当年的叫声还回荡
在仙女山的山坳中
但这里是汨罗
几头牛正在不远处的草甸上
安详地吃草
我的牛喷着鼻息
茫然四顾
一会儿哞哞
一会儿咩咩
一会儿喔喔
像找不到声带的我
在这首诗的尽头
眼巴巴看着
绿水从青山经过

In Miluo
Lan Lan asked me
if I could moo like a cow
Lan's voice hardly fell
before a cow
ran out from my rib cage
This cow could not moo
Perhaps she once had
perhaps her moo still reverberated
in the valley of Xiannv Mountain
but we were in Miluo
In a nearby meadow a few cows were
grazing peacefully
My cow snorted
eyes wandering all around
moo moo
mie mie
wo wo
like a voiceless me
at the end of this poem
hopelessly eyeing
green waters flowing away from green mountains

什么是飞禽，什么是走兽

我的小狗永远不明白它属于哪儿
与猫争夺耗子
与麻雀争抢草坪
今天晌午，为驱逐一只苍蝇
它一头撞上了仙人球
在给它拔刺的时候
它眼睛里有我
在我心目中，它人模狗样
自由与禁锢挤压出
这样一个泪汪汪的怪物
既勇敢又怯懦。我的小狗不明白
飞禽有飞禽的弹道
走兽有走兽的迷途
而裂开的人缝不是为了便于它穿梭
是为了对应天上的那些窟窿
那些被我们误以为是出路的
大悲伤

BIRDS VS. BEASTS

My little dog has never figured out where she belonged
chasing mice in competition with cats
and fighting for the turf with sparrows
This noon, to drive away a fly
she rammed into a cactus
Drawing out the needles for her
I saw my reflection in her eyes
Deep down, I feel she likes to pretend to be what she is not
Freedom and fetter have turned out
such a tearful monster
brave and cowardly. My little dog does not understand
birds have their trajectories
beasts have their routes
and the narrow passes for people may not be easy paths
for her
Mirroring holes in the sky
they are not escapes as we think of them
they are catastrophes

一杆秤

杀牛的那天下午
我们坐在田坎上把玩一杆秤
漆黑油腻的秤杆上
有一串白色的模糊的星星
秤钩又亮又尖
秤砣又大又沉
全村的人都来了
欢天喜地
围着一口大铁锅
杀牛的那天下午
我们在沸腾的铁锅旁
央求屠夫
将我们每个人都挂在铁钩上
称一称
当我蜷起腿离开地面时
我第一次知道了
自己的斤两

A STEELYARD

On the afternoon to slaughter the buffalo
we sat on the field ridge playing with a steelyard
The dark and greasy arm of the scale
had a string of fuzzy white stars
The hook was shining and pointed
and the counterweight, huge and heavy
All the villagers showed up
in high spirits
and surrounded the vast iron cauldron
On the afternoon to slaughter the buffalo
beside the boiling cauldron we
begged the butcher
to put each of us on the hook
to weigh our weight
When I curled up to detach from the ground
for the first time I got to know
my own worth

修地球的人

清晨他们出门
带上畚箕、锄头和锹
也带走了门前的大雾
当他们成群结队消失
在屋后的山岗上
我们背上书包迎着太阳跑
傍晚他们回家
把沉重的畚箕、锄头和锹
放下，一言不发
阴暗的房间安静得可怕
只有月亮明白无误地
照耀着地球上的一个
角落。我在角落削铅笔
用余光打量日复一日的生活
山那边有一座坑
他们越挖越深
我希望那将是我们的逃生通道

THOSE WHO FIX THE EARTH

They depart in the morning
with bamboo woven dustpans, hoes, and shovels
taking the fog in front of the gate with them as well
As they disappear in groups
up the hill behind the house
we carry our schoolbags and run towards the sun
They return in the evening
their heavy dustpans, hoes, and shovels
laid down; they are silent
the dark rooms appear terribly quiet
only the moon unequivocally
shines on the earth's
one corner. I am sharpening my pencil
and measuring with the eye the routine of life
On the other side of the hill is a pit
they've been digging deeper and deeper
I hope that will be our escape route

烟花表演

FIREWORKS SHOW

回老家的山坡上找
一种叫柞木的树蔸
用老家的洋镐把它挖出来
放在太阳下暴晒
如果父亲还活着
他会一如既往
在岁末的星空下等我
他会把火钳递到我手上
让我敲打燃烧的树蔸
噼啪作响的烟花在空中飞舞
那是我见过的
最灿烂的夜空
当我在记忆中使劲敲打
残存的木头隐约可见
灰烬中的父亲一明一灭
明的时候山河屈指可数
灭的时候世界漆黑
我也深陷其中

I went back to my hometown to find on the slope
a stump of an oak tree
I dug it up with our family's pickaxe
and dried it in the sun
Had my father been alive
he would as usual
wait for me under the starry sky
He would put the tongs in my hand
and urge me to strike the burning stump
The crackling sparks would dance in the air
and to me that would be
the most splendid night sky
When I struck hard the pickaxe in my mind
the remaining stump became almost visible
and my father flashed on and off in ashes
when on, just a few mountains and rivers were discernible
when off, the world turned pitch black
with me deep in darkness

暮色四合之地 TWILIGHT COURTYARD

很难再见暮色四合之地了
晚风徐徐，晚霞淡去
亲人们在鸡飞狗跳中归来
父亲蹲在水边先擦拭农具，再将
洗净的脚塞进湿滑的鞋帮里
母亲把干透的衣服拢成一堆
扔进姐姐们的怀中
很难再见我那么肮脏的脸上
浮现出来的干净和轻盈
只有黑暗在无声无息中包围住我们
却不知房间里的光从哪里亮起

It is hard to find that twilight courtyard again
Evening breeze puffing, sunset glow fading
my folks returned from a hectic day
Dad squatted near water, wiping his farm tools before
putting his cleansed feet back into his slippery shoes
Mom gathered the air-dried clothes into a heap
and passed them onto the embrace of my sisters
It is hard to find again my dirty face
that beamed with purity and freshness
when only darkness soundlessly surrounds us
and no way to know where light will brighten up the room

无主之树

NOBODY'S TREE

如何判断一棵树
是病死的还是老死的
在人迹罕至的原始森林
我常常会陷入盲从
病死也罢老死也好
总归死得其所
但在我的家乡有这样一棵梨树
孤零零地长在门前
百米开外的田埂旁
树干粗大，树枝旁逸斜出
春天开过多少花
夏天就结多少果
而到了秋天路过的人
蹿上枝梢随意采摘
一年又一年
我们都以为它会一直这样活
尤其是在我远离家乡几十年后
还好几次在梦中见过它
但事实上它已经死去多年
没有人告诉过我
它因何而死就像没人知道
它为什么而活，孤零零的
像花圈之于填满灰烬的坟墓

To diagnose if a tree
died of disease or naturally
in the untrodden primeval forest
I often follow blindly
Either way
it's a fair death
But in my hometown, there was such a pear tree
standing alone in front of a gate
around a hundred meters away from the fields
its trunk massive and branches sticking out in all directions
The amount of flowering it had in spring
meant an equal amount of fruiting in summer
In autumn passersby would
climb onto it to harvest at will
Year after year
we all thought it would live like this forever
Even after leaving my hometown for decades
I still saw it several times in my dreams
Yet the truth is, it died years ago
Nobody told me
why it died just like nobody told me
why it had lived; lonely
it existed like a funeral wreath to a tomb of ashes

室韦的祷告

SHIWEI'S PRAYER

神呐，就把我流放到这里吧
抽空我的人性
在我体内灌注更多的蛮力和无知
让我在河谷中替你啃食草屑
让我和那些大鸨一样随心所欲地
在你的天空中翻飞
再也没有国籍，没有
被铁丝网圈起来的该死的爱憎

Oh, God, let me exile here
Extract my humanity
and instill more brute force and ignorance in me
Let me graze the grass in the valleys for you
Let me be free like the great bustards
and soar in your sky
No more nationality, no
love and hate damned and behind barbed wire

风在竹林里干什么 WHAT IS THE WIND DOING IN THE BAMBOO FOREST

种很多竹子
等它们长成竹林
在竹林深处建一栋木屋
门前留一条路通往河边
门后留一条路通往后山
我计划退休以后去那里长住
而现在我仍然住在这里
眼前的竹子都是后来栽上的
眼前的路也非我所修
春雷就要响了
吃笋子的季节就要到了
我在竹园边避风
听见竹林里传来嘤嘤声
那一定是北风迷路了
抱着竹竿在哭
像人到中年的我一样
空怀一腔愿望却举步维艰

Plant lots of bamboo
and see them grow into a forest
Build a wooden cottage deep there
leave a path in the front to lead to the river
and leave another behind to reach the back mountain
I plan after retirement to stay there for long
But for now I still live where I am
All the bamboo was planted after I had moved in
nor was the road constructed by me
Spring thunder is about to roar
so is the season for eating bamboo shoots around the corner
I've retreated to the bamboo grove
Hearing weeping from it
I surmise the north wind has lost its way
It holds onto a bamboo cane and cries
much like middle-aged me
full of wishes yet floundering

在景迈山深处仰望星空

AN UPWARD LOOK AT THE STARRY SKY DEEP IN JINGMAI MOUNTAIN

连续三个晚上我们头顶繁星
活在景迈山深处
漆黑的夜色助长了星空的浩大
仿佛大地上的事物越是渺小
我们越是能够明了宇宙的结构
造物主有自己的建筑学
每一颗星星都像图钉
把它的意图钉在我们的头顶
任由我们指认
金星在缅甸闪烁
白矮星今夜在越南——
从我笔立的食指往上看
童年时给我启蒙的北斗似乎迷了路
银河两岸浪花四溅
星空越是喧哗我们越是沉默
在黑暗中保持住婴儿的动作

Stars overhead, for three nights in a row
we stayed deep in Jingmai Mountain
The pitch-dark night enlarged the starry sky
as if the smaller everything on earth was
the more we could grasp the universe's structure
The creator had his own architecture
each star like a thumbtack
pinning His will over our head
allowing us to point and identify
Venus twinkling over Myanmar
White Dwarf passing the night above Vietnam—
Looking up straight from my index finger
the North Star that once enlightened me seemed to have
lost its way
Waves splashed on either side of the Milky Way
the noisier the star-dotted sky the more silent we were
In darkness we maintained the pose of an infant

荷叶上的青蛙

FROG ON A LOTUS LEAF

一只青蛙蹲在荷叶上
荷叶倾斜着
一滴水珠在荷叶上
来回滚动
夏天过了一半
难过仍未结束
像青蛙一样蹲着
像水珠一样无疾而终
像荷叶一样慌张
像荷叶上的青蛙在雷雨中
不敢大声鸣叫
我也不敢说出
我想干什么又能干什么

A frog squats on a lotus leaf
the leaf leans
On the leaf a drop of water
rolls back and forth
Summer is half gone
yet the unbearable is yet to end
Squat like the frog
disappear like the drop of water
panic like the lotus leaf
like the frog on the lotus leaf in a thunderstorm
afraid to croak loudly
I dare not to say
what I want to and can do

认领

THE CLAIM

春分过后阳气回升
伸懒腰的人也拉抻着驼背
走在路上时常感觉
这也可以有
那也是自己的
尤其是在黄昏
逆光中的少女忽走忽停
像一个个忽近忽远的发光体
婆娑的季节就要到了
路边的香樟树要在风中
抖落一些旧叶
才能为新芽腾出空枝

After the spring equinox Yang Qi increases
and he who stretches also straightens the bent back
Walking on the road he often feels
he can have this
and that also belongs to him
particularly during the dusk
Girls facing the light walk and pause and walk again
like many a glowing entity
It's soon the season for thriving trees
In the wind the roadside camphor trees must
shake off some old leaves
to surrender branches to fresh sprouts

逆行

WALK TOWARDS EACH OTHER

一个女孩逆行的时候往往会低着头
但一群女孩逆行时她们会逼迫你低下头去
一群女孩迎面走来像一串音符
在跳荡，却不拘囿于五线谱
再宽的马路也是拥挤的
再趾高气扬的男人都不在话下
昨天下午我跟在他身后
看着他越来越稀疏的后脑勺
太阳就要落山了
我有点想哭

One girl walking in your direction would lower her head
One group of girls would force you to lower your head
One group of girls walking is like a series of musical notes
cavorting, refusing to stay in boundaries of the staff
the widest road is too crowded
the most arrogant man can be conquered
Yesterday afternoon I followed him
the back of his balding head in view
The sun was about to set
I felt like crying

来访者

THE VISITOR

来访的斑鸠在窗外
的樟树上探头探脑
来访的鸽子站在窗台上
朝我的书房里面瞅
来访的风掀了掀窗帘
却不进屋
我伸出手恰好遇到了来访的手
从门外递进来的光
我握住它的时候感觉到
它正在往回抽

The visiting turtledove outside the window
on the camphor tree pokes its head in and looks about
The visiting pigeon stands on the windowsill
peeping into my study
The visiting wind lifts the curtain
but does not enter
I extend my hand and luckily grab the visiting hand
that delivers light from the outside
When I hold it I feel
it is pulling back

空欢喜

REJOICED TOO SOON

左边有水杉
右边是樟木
晨光临近了
我乐在其中
我乐于靠在枕头上
怀抱另外一个枕头
想象你也是这样
扭头看着窗外的春风
一会儿蹑手蹑脚
一会儿探头探脑
如果我们都不看它
它就会使劲地
摇晃树梢直到
把一只鸟摇下天空

Redwood trees on the left
Camphorwood trees on the right
Dawn was breaking
I was enjoying the moment
leaning on one pillow
and holding another in my arms
I pictured you were like me
turning to look at the spring breeze outside the window
one moment it tiptoed
another it sneaked around
When neither of us were looking
it would vigorously
shake the treetops till
a bird fell from the air

睡前故事

BEDTIME STORY

最好听的故事讲到一半
会遇到睡眠；最平静的
呼吸里浮现过一张
从来没有见过的脸
最好看的人不是别人
也许就是你了——你
俯身在床头像
一本摊开的连环画
折痕处往往是故事的低谷
我曾是最好的听众
在没有人见过的黑暗中
我曾是最好的读者
在无人入睡的晚上
最好听的故事从前发生过
今后还会继续
今后还将由我向你转述

The finest story will yield halfway
to sleep; the calmest
breath will give way to
an unseen face
The most attractive is nobody
but you—your body
leaning against the bed as if
an open picture book
and its fold, the anticlimax
I used to be your best audience
against unprecedented darkness
I was once your best reader
during sleepless nights
The finest story took place already
yet it continues from now
and I shall retell it to you later on

泡木耳

你不知道我有多喜欢木耳
你没见过
每当我把它们浸泡在水里时
我们同时心满意足的样子
像刚从梦中醒来伸伸懒腰
侧身望着窗外
昨晚又下过雨了
现在雨过天晴
木耳趴在湿漉漉的枝丫上
静静地聆听水滴
落在腐叶上的声音
你不知道我也曾这样
沉浸在遗世的欢乐中
以为我们都能像木耳这样
逆来顺受，生生不息
以为这世上最动听的声音
是我热泪盈眶地抱着熟睡的你
却终于忍不住
落在你脸上的泪滴声

REHYDRATING WOOD EAR MUSHROOMS

You don't know how much I like wood ear mushrooms
You haven't seen
whenever I soak them in water
the satisfactory look on both of us
It's as if just waking up from dreams, stretching
and turning to look outside the window
Last night it rained again
now the sky has cleared up
Mushrooms are lying on wet boughs
listening quietly to waterdrops
falling onto rotten leaves
You don't know I once also
immersed in this joy of staying free of the world
believing all could be like the mushrooms
accepting, growing, and multiplying without end
believing the most beautiful sounds in this world
are those of my tears falling onto your face
as an excited me holding a sound-asleep you
could not hold them back anymore

树叶走路的声音

THE SOUND OF LEAVES WALKING

树叶在空中走动时
你不一定留心过
嫩绿是一步
枯黄是另外一大步
你在树下来回奔波
直到一片叶子落下来
一树落叶在秋风中形成旋涡
你抬头时看见
天空已经发生了变化
从前长满树叶的枝丫上
落满了不知从哪里飞来的鸟
到了晚上，凌晨时分
大地上全是树叶的走动声
它们从树下跑到墙根下
它们集合又分散，分散又集合
像一群走投无路的人
走着走着
就消逝在了道路尽头

When leaves walk in the air
you may not have noticed
verdant is one step
brown and bare another
You run about under the tree
until one leaf falls
until all leaves from the tree swirl in the autumn wind
When you look up
you realized the air has altered
branches once laden with leaves
are now dotted with birds from nowhere
At night and early morning
the ground is full of footfalls of leaves
moving from underneath trees to corners of walls
The leaves gather and scatter, scatter and gather
like a bunch of desperate people
rushing about
and then vanishing at the end of the road

心里话

FROM THE BOTTOM OF MY HEART

好久没见太阳了
今天特别想她
像想念你一样想她
像已经忘记了你一样
我忘记了
你现世的模样
和你不在世时
我难过的形状

Haven't seen the sun for quite a while
Today I miss her terribly
much like I miss you
As if I have already forgotten you
I have forgotten
your present look
and when you are no longer around
the sad look of myself

像样的爱情	HEART ON FIRE
一起看花的两个人或	Two people going to see flowers together and
两个人一起看花	a couple seeing flowers together
并不是同一件事	are not the same
譬如说杜鹃花开了	Let's say when azaleas bloom
失火的山谷里并不见救火的人	and no firefighters are there to rescue the valley from a fire
两个人在火海中不知所措	and the couple in flames are stunned
你看我我看你	They would look at each other
越看越觉得此生可惜	The more they do it the more they feel regret
这样的爱谁不想要呢	Who does not long for such love
这样的爱至死不见骨灰	such love that transcends ashes

红桦树

RED BIRCH

娥嫚沟的尽头有两棵红桦树	Deep in Eman valley were two red birches
在摆脱了其他树木的纠缠后	Disentangled from the other trees
它们越长越像红桦树了	they grew more and more like their own kind
这两棵天荒地老的红桦树	These two trees of eternity
早晚都等候在天池旁	from dawn to dusk stood by Tianchi Lake
沐浴在天荒地老的喜悦中	indulgent in the joy of eternity
除了它们，没有人知道	Nobody, except they, knew
娥嫚沟的尽头在哪里	the depth of the valley
没有人能像红桦树那样	and nobody could like these two
与天荒地老为伍	stay so close to eternity

跳出油锅的鱼

吃过那么多的鱼，印象最深的
却是那条没有吃进嘴里的——
它从滚烫的油锅里跳了出去
——在我目瞪口呆的瞬间
鱼鳞、腮、内脏又迅速长回身体
现在我相信它完好无损地
回到了它熟悉的水域
像什么都没有发生过一样
春天产籽，夏天浮出水面呼吸
秋天到了，它仍旧会游到鱼钩附近
在不舍得与不甘心之间打漩
命运在轮回，我对此深信不疑
我深信油锅并非万能
煎熬不过是轮回的一部分

FISH THAT JUMPED OUT OF THE OIL PAN

Among all the fish I have eaten, the most impressive
is the one I did not actually get to eat—
It jumped out of a pan of boiling oil
—While I stood dumbfounded
its scales, gills, and internal organs quickly grew back
I now believe the fish returned intact
to its familiar waters
as if nothing had happened
spawning in spring, floating to the surface for air in summer
when autumn comes, it would swim close to bait again
vacillating between desire and discontent
I firmly believe Fate to be reincarnation
I don't believe a frying pan is omnipotent
suffering is but a part of reincarnation

汇合

如果没有风
玉兰树的叶子永远没有机会
与香樟树的叶子在大地上相逢
当它们在暮春的清晨
被两把笤帚扫到一起
如果不是因为身处困境
笤帚的主人可能不是他们
每天清晨我听见楼下传来
笤帚划过大地的刺啦声
女的从楼后，男的从楼前
它们汇合的时候曾有过片刻的宁静
之后像久别重逢的人
高声谈论着各自的见闻
如果落叶能听懂他俩的方言
就不会奇怪造物主的安排
两把笤帚在清扫完成之后
被归并到了蓝色的垃圾桶内
如果此时我还能入睡
一定是因为我太孤单了
已经接受了被人类抛弃的理由

MEETING EACH OTHER

Were it not for the wind
the leaf of the magnolia tree would never
meet that of the camphor tree on the ground
on that morning of a late spring when they
were swept together by two brooms
Were it not for some difficult situations
the owners of the brooms would not have
been this pair—
each morning I heard downstairs
brooms swishing across the ground
the woman sweeping behind the building and
the man, front
There would be a moment of quietness when
they met
Then as if reunited after a long separation
they loudly shared what they had seen and heard
Were the leaves to understand human dialects
the leaves would not be surprised by nature's
arrangement
After the two brooms completed the cleaning
they were put together into the blue trash can
Were I still able to fall asleep
my loneliness must have been so intense
that I've accepted why the world abandoned
me

同类的忧伤

两个惺惺相惜的男人
各自拿着一把铲子
蹲在地球上找土
这是夏日的正午
连鸟雀都在午休
地球上仿佛只剩下了他们俩
唉声叹气的声音
从这里到那里
又折回到这里
蹲在围墙边的树篱下
他们开始挖
足足半个小时之后
才直起腰来
拎起一只黑色的塑料袋
正要离开
我迎了上去看见
袋子里装满了混凝土和碎石
三个惺惺相惜的男人
穿过滚烫大地
来到楼顶平台
一只空洞的陶盆外沿上兰草茂盛
盆里放着几株奄奄一息的菜苗
他们把袋中土倒进盆内
轮换着用铲子捣鼓
从平台尽头望过去
故乡只剩下了一个方位
三个男人和几株幼苗
站在夏日正午的楼顶上
如果此时有第四个人来到这里
如果有更多的人来到这里
围绕在这只陶盆旁
这算不算得上同类的忧伤

THE SAME KIND OF SADNESS

Two like-minded men
shovels in their hands
squatted on the ground
It's a summer afternoon
even birds were napping
As if the last two creatures on earth
the men moaned and groaned
moving from here to there
and then back
Bending under the hedge near a wall
they started to dig
After a good half an hour
did they stand straight
holding a black plastic bag
ready to leave
I approached them and found
concrete and gravel in the bag
Three like-minded men
walked on the burning ground
and onto a rooftop
Orchids bloomed on the rim of a clay pot
But inside only a few vegetables barely alive
The men emptied the bag, filled up the pot
and took turns to break up the rubble
Far away from the rooftop
their hometown has been reduced to only a
direction
Three men and a few seedlings
stood this summer noon on a rooftop
If at that point a fourth man had come by
if more people had come
to surround this pot
would it be counted as the same kind of sadness

尺度

我父亲喜欢用手指拃量树木
家具、衣服、身高和田畴……
拃过之后他会感觉这双手还有用
他迷信自己的手如同木匠
迷信那一截蘸了墨汁的绳索
弹在木板上的声音是有形状的
我兄弟买了一段软皮尺供我母亲
剪裁衣服用，每到腊月时
缝纫机半夜还在响，可我
整个童年都没有穿过几件新衣服
我兄弟有一支木制大三角板
涂了黄漆，刻度是黑色的
他在摊开的报纸上画几何图
但他从来不相信人能垂直于大地上
后来他当了父亲依然驼着背
他儿子也不相信这么大的三角板有什么用
他买了一把卷尺闪闪发亮
他丈过自己的庭院，和前途
但很快就缩了回去
而我几乎是双手空空地来到了
没有他们存在的地方
没有土地，树木，没有庭院
我活在被人丈量过的生活中
常常随手拿起身边的各种尺子
体味着尺有所长之苦
如果我的父亲现在还活着
他一定能丈量出我们之间的距离
在他手指成灰之前也许他已经
在心里丈量过了，不然的话
为什么总有人在耳边提醒我：
“不要相信你无法抚摸的生活。”

THE SPAN

My father liked to measure trees with his fingers
furniture, clothes, human height, and fields…
Afterwards he would feel his hands still useful
He believed in his hands as much as carpenters
believed that the sound of ink line
tapped on wood boards has shape
My brother bought a sewing tape for my mother
to make clothes; each December
the sewing machine whirred even at midnight,
    but I
had barely worn any new clothes throughout my
    childhood
My brother owned a large wood triangle ruler
painted in yellow, marked in black metrics
He drew geometric shapes on spread out
    newspapers
but never believed man can stand
    perpendicular to the vast land
Even after he became a father his back still
    hunched
Neither did my nephew believe in the large set
    square
He bought a shining tape measure
to estimate his homestead, his future
but quickly backed out
Whereas, almost barehandedly I came to
where they were the nonexistent
where I had no land, trees, nor yard
I live a life measured by others
often fathoming varied scales of measurement at
    hand
and suffering from great lengths
Were my father still alive
he would be able to measure the distance
    between him and me
Perhaps before his fingers turned ashes he had
    already
done it in his mind; otherwise
why do I always hear a voice reminding me:
Do not believe what you cannot touch

我见过黄鹤

现在轮到我讲述
这里曾经发生过
什么。轮到我
用朗诵腔赞美
那只并不存在的
大鸟：啊它高飞
又低徊，一次次
掠过了汉阳树和
鹦鹉洲——从来都是
这样：我们活在低处
却轻易就拥有了
眺望的视觉，自以为
见多识广，一次次
化身为洒脱的辜负
啊 大江日夜流
回不去与归不得的
哀愁，从来都是
由空濛的天际来传导
而我不过是在心底
悄然把方言兑换成了
一杯浓烈的和泪酒
——饮罢下扬州
千里不回头——
但听得一声长啸盘旋
在每一条出口的尽头
你挥一挥衣袖就接受了
越来越平缓浑浊的江流

I'VE SEEN THE YELLOW CRANE

Now it's my turn to tell
what once happened
here, my turn to
use a celebratory tone to extol
that non-existent
big bird: Oh, it soars
or wanders low, again and again
over the Hanyang Tree and
Parrot Isle—It's always
like this: Low in position
we easily adopt
an upward look, taking for granted
our experiences, and again and again
embody disappointment
Oh, the river flows day and night
unable to return or reverse its course
the attendant sorrow has always been
conveyed through the firmament
All I do is deep in my heart
exchanging my dialect quietly for
a shot of liquor mixed with tears
—With that I head for Yangzhou
and over hundreds of miles never turn my head—
as I hear a shout hovering
over the end of each exit
You waved and easily submitted to
the ever-flattening turbid flow

更好的人

晨起熬粥的人在鸟鸣声中
喝下粥，他清楚地听见
送奶工把手伸进了奶箱盒
晨起看日出的人在山顶的浓雾里
眺望浓雾，哦浓雾
晨起讨生活，终究还是晚了
更好的生活已经名花有主
更多的人像我一样
在梦里艰难地挪动
更好的人配得上这样的
一天——既新鲜又世俗
他将在碌碌无为中享用
身体里塞满了懊恼与满足
他配得上这样的白日梦
谁也不会去打搅他
他也不会去说服谁

A BETTER PERSON

He who got up early to make congee heard birds chirping
while finishing the breakfast; he heard clearly
when the milkman reached for the milk crates
He who got up early to see sunrise stood in heavy fog on
the hilltop
and gazed into heavy fog. Oh, heavy fog
I started early to make a living, but still end up being late
Better life was already taken
Most people are like me
plodding in dreams
A better person deserves such
a day—fresh and prosaic
He will enjoy it in a busy yet insignificant manner
much to his chagrin and satisfaction
He befits such a daydream
Nobody will disturb him
Nobody will he try to persuade

篇五 我们怎么能区分舞蹈和跳舞人？

V. *How can we know the dancer from the dance?*

南瓜长大了 THE PUMPKIN IS GROWING BIG

南瓜长大了就会找一个地方蹲下来	When a pumpkin grows sizable it finds a spot to squat down
静静地孵它的瓤	and quietly nurtures the pulp
我也是这样	So do I
在把田埂走穿之后就坐在半山腰上	by sitting halfway up on a hill after I passed the fields
新堆与旧坟在我身后起伏	new and old tombs undulating behind me
岩子河在不远处闪光	the Yanzi River shimmering nearby
更近的地方是一些无名的草木	and even closer some unknown vegetation standing
热浪翻涌，虫豸也厌倦了鸣叫	Heat waves surging, even insects feel too weary to chirp
没有什么真正的沧桑	There are no real great changes
只有该熟的熟了该死的死了	What should ripen ripens, and what should die dies
活在我眼中的填满了我内心的空洞	Those alive in front of me fill up the hollow inside

奔跑的雨

RUNNING RAIN

回头看看那个烧成了灰烬的夏天
我们也曾被暴雨追赶
并无征兆但事先得到过乌云的警告
我们漂浮在滚烫的河面上
仰望云破处，想象有朝一日
生活也会被镶上金边
就在那时，一阵旋风踮起脚尖
沿着堤坝朝榨油坊那边跑过来
掳走了我们放在河堤上的衣物
回头看看那些浪花越溅越高了
有人飞快地游到了岸边
手指黑压压的雨幕目瞪口呆
一群赤条条的少年站在岸上
巨大的雨仗即将经过岩子河
冲到最前面的雨点追上了
跑得最快的我。回头看看我吧
那被暴雨砸中的样子
像一块滋滋冒气的顽石
没有燃烧过也没有熄灭过

Looking back to that burnt up summer
we were once caught in a rainstorm too
without forecast but warned by dark clouds
We floated on the scorching river
gazing at the break in the clouds, imagining one day
to also have a gilded life
Then, a gust of whirlwind tiptoed
along the riverbank towards the oil mill and us
looting along its way our clothing
Seeing the waves rising higher and higher
some of us quickly swam ashore
pointing at the stunning dark curtain of rain
A line of naked young men standing along the shore
witnessed a major downpour to battle the Yanzi River
The quickest raindrops came down
on me the fastest runner. In reminiscences
I who was hit by the rain was like
a steaming stone
neither burnt nor extinguished

中午吃什么

我还没有灶台高的时候
总是喜欢踮着脚尖
站在母亲身前朝锅里瞅
冒着热气的大锅
盖上了木盖的大锅
我喜欢问她中午吃什么
安静的厨房里
柴火燃烧的声音也是安静的
厨房外面，太阳正在天井上面燃烧
我帮母亲摆好碗筷之后
就在台阶上安静地坐着
等候家人一个一个进屋
他们也喜欢问中午吃什么

WHAT'S FOR LUNCH

Before I was tall enough to reach the stovetop
I liked to stand on tiptoes
in front of my mom to check out the wok
the giant steaming wok
the giant wok covered by a wooden lid
I liked to ask her what's for lunch
In the quiet kitchen
the burning of the firewood was also quiet
Outside the kitchen, the sun shone above the patio
After helping my mom set the table
I would sit quietly on the doorstep
waiting for the rest of my family to file into the room
They also liked to ask what's for lunch

捡鸡蛋 COLLECTING CHICKEN EGGS

天黑之前最后一件事	Before darkness fell the last chore
由我来干：捡鸡蛋	was mine: to collect the chicken eggs
搬两块砖头垫在脚下	I would place two bricks under my feet
我终于够到了鸡窝了	to finally reach the nests
摸遍每一个角落	I would search each and every corner
把鸡蛋轻轻放进葫芦瓢	and put the eggs gently into a gourd scoop
惊惶的鸡笼这才彻底安静了下来	When the startled chickens completely calmed down
我跨进门槛返身插上门闩	I would cross the threshold and latch the door behind me
仍有凉意从门缝挤进屋	though coldness still seeped through the cracks
我从来没有告诉过父母	I never told my parents
那一刻我的心跳有多快	how wildly my heart pounded at that moment

草垛 HAYSTACK

我钻进草垛	I climbed into the haystack
在草垛里打洞	burrowed
碰见了	and saw
鸡蛋，和石头	an egg, and a rock
冬天多么暖和	That winter was so warm
鸡在草垛上争食	chickens were fighting for food on the haystack
大人们在外面生活	grown-ups were going about their business outside the haystack
我在草垛里爬来爬去	I was crawling around in the haystack
在草垛尽头遇见你	until in the other end of it I ran into you
一手拿着鸡蛋	egg in one hand
一手拿着石头	rock in the other

摇窝	BASSINET
一个女人坐在摇窝旁	A woman sat beside the bassinet
用手，用脚	her hand, foot
用膝盖、胳膊肘	knee, elbow
用身体的任意部位	or any part of her body
触碰摇窝	gently rocking it
只要摇窝晃动	As long as the bassinet was moving
世界就是安静的	the world was peaceful
我见过这个女人	I had seen this woman
我见识过安静的生活	I had experienced this peaceful life
阳光穿过我们头顶的楝树	The sunlight overhead shone through the chinaberry
树叶颤抖而楝果沉着	The leaves shook but the fruit kept calm
有人路过这棵树	Someone walked past the tree
站在天空打量我	looking down at me
有人在远方喊她	Someone far away called her
她放下毛线活儿直起身来	She put down her knitting and rose from her seat
摇窝依然在晃动	The bassinet remained moving

阳光真好

GOOD SUNSHINE

洗净的衣服拧干后
要在空中抖开
一个人能干的活无需两个人合作
我在树阴下睡觉
阳光真好
只晒那些需要晒的
妈妈你真好
不把床单洗干净你不会叫醒我
而当我醒来
我会像泥鳅一样灵活
抓紧床单的一角
旋转着身体，使劲拧
你在那一头咯咯地笑
我在这一头越拧越起劲
到现在仍然不肯松手

After washing and wringing
the clothes should lie flat to air dry
One person's work did not need two pairs of hands
I was sleeping under the shade of the tree
Good sunshine
only those needing airdry would be dried
Good mom
you would not wake me up until work was done
When I did wake up
I would be as nimble as an eel
holding one end of a bedsheet
rolling myself, and squeezing hard the laundry
and you would giggle on the other end
The longer I rolled the more excited I became
so much so that I would not let it go even now

冬青树

THE HOLLY TREE

我在冬青树上睡了一宿	I slept overnight in a holly
那年我五岁	That year I was five
被父亲赶上了冬青树	Chased by my father up into the tree
我抱着树干唱了一会儿歌	I held the tree and sang for a while
夜鸟在竹林里振翅	nocturnal birds flapping their wings in the bamboo grove
我安静的时候它们也安静了下来	When I quieted down, so did they
我们都安静的时候	When we were all quiet
只有月亮在天上奔走	only the moon rushed about in the sky
只有妈妈倚着门框在哭	only my mother wept against the door frame

夜晚的习惯

我至今还保持着
用热水烫脚的习惯
只是木盆换成了电热桶
当我做这件事的时候
一天已近尾声
我把双脚伸进热水
就想起当年的那些夜晚
我被母亲摁在木盆边
若是水太烫了
我就大喊大叫
小个子的母亲像犯了错一样
忙不迭地跑到水缸旁
抓起木瓢
舀一勺凉水倒进盆中
我想起她
总是仰头望着我
边兑水边用手搅拌着
从前我总爱先洗左脚
把右脚搭在她的膝盖上
不像现在，我总是默默地
把双脚同时伸进去
再同时抽出来

NIGHT HABIT

I still keep the habit of
soaking my feet in warm water
though an electric tub has replaced a wood one
When it happens
the day usually is drawing to an end
Dipping my feet into the warm water
I would recall those nights
when my mother pressed my feet to the rim of the tub
If the water was too hot
I would scream loudly
My petite mother, as if she had made a mistake
rush to the water vat
grab the wood ladle
and add a scoop of cold water into the tub
In my memory
she was always looking upward to me
while stirring the water
I liked to first soak my left foot
while resting my right on her lap
Unlike then, I am now used to quietly
putting both feet into the water
and drawing them out at the same time

后视镜 REAR—VIEW MIRROR

在长途班车的后视镜中	In the rear-view mirror of the long-distance shuttle bus
越来越小的黑影	the gradually shrinking black dot
由刍狗变成了蝼蚁	morphed from a humble dog into an ant
命运的盘山路眼看着	Fate's winding road was visibly
就要到达山顶了	reaching its summit
从窗口探出头去	I poked my head out of the window
镜子里面还有一个人	and saw another person in the mirror
长发被风卷到了窗外	Long hair blown outside the window
此时她正朝山脚下眺望	she was gazing down towards the foot of the mountain
那里曾经有过一座村庄	There was once a village
班车经过时尘土飞扬	which witnessed dust when a bus passed
班车经过后它消失在了尘土中	and disappeared in dust when a bus was gone
我习惯倚靠窗沿漠然地看着	I habitually leaned against the window and stared indifferently at
几十年前的那一幕	that scene of decades ago
——我的母亲高举双臂	—My mother held both of her arms high
在尘埃中挥舞	waving in dust
最后又无可奈何放下臂膀	putting them down helplessly
垂头丧气扑打着衣襟	and then brushing her lapel dejectedly

如果根茎能说话　IF THE ROOT COULD SPEAK

如果根茎能说话
它会先说黑暗，再说光明
它会告诉你：黑暗中没有国家
光明中不分你我
这里是潮湿的，那里干燥
蚯蚓穿过一座孤坟大概需要半生
而蚂蚁爬上树顶只是为了一片叶芽
如果根茎能说话
它会说地下比地上好
死去的母亲仍然活着
今年她十一岁了
十一年来我只见过一次她
如果根茎继续说
它会说到我小时候曾坐在树下
拿一把铲子，对着地球
轻轻地挖

If the root could speak
it would first speak of darkness, and then brightness
It would tell you: In darkness there is no country
Brightness does not differentiate you and me
Here is humid and there, dry
It takes about half of an earthworm's life to traverse a lone tomb
The ant climbs up to the treetop merely for a leaf
If the root could speak
it would say underground is better than aboveground
My deceased mother still lives
This year she is turning eleven
I have only seen her once during these eleven years
If the root continued to speak
it would recall a little me sitting under a tree
holding a spade, facing the ground
gently digging

樟脑丸

为什么春天的衣服
可以放到秋天穿而夏天的
衣服冬天却不能穿?
请问樟脑丸:
冬青树都落叶了为什么
窗前的香樟树还绿着?
我母亲坐在那口脱漆的
木箱里面叠衣服
叠完了衣服
就消逝在了箱子中

MOTHBALLS

Why can spring clothes
be stored for autumn use while summer
clothes are not good for winter?
Dear mothballs:
Why has the holly lost its leaves
but the camphor tree in front of the window is still green?
My mother was sitting in a paint-stripped
wooden box folding laundry
Once finished
she disappeared into the box

有一次

有一次我决定
自己动手缝一枚纽扣
打开针线盒
找到了针和线
我来到窗边找到了
线头，和针孔
我一次次调换针线的角度
以为自己不会认输
有一次我决定
不再帮妈妈穿针了
我厌倦了需要她照顾的生活
我以为我已经赢得了生活
再也用不着为一枚
掉落的纽扣发愁
有一次我衬衣上的第三颗纽扣掉了
我拿着纽扣在书桌上转动
母亲在桌前的相框里微笑
她以为我永远不会服输

ONCE

Once I decided
to sew a button myself
Opening the sewing kit
picking out the suitable needle and thread
I walked to the window to pinpoint
the thread end and the eye of the needle
I adjusted again and again the thread and needle
taking for granted that I would not fail
Once I decided
to no longer help my mother thread a needle
I was tired of being coddled by her
I thought I had already won over life
no longer needing to
worry over a missing button
Once the third button on my shirt fell off
I turned the button on my desk
my mother smiling in the portrait above the desk
She thought I would never admit failing

茄子 EGGPLANT

能使人发笑的蔬菜似乎只有茄子	The only vegetable that can make one laugh is the eggplant
无论是白茄子还是紫茄子	white or purple
当你喊“茄子”——笑容	When you shout *qiezi*, the sound of the words—a smile
就会出现在脸上	pops up on your face
这有点像我的母亲	This situation reminds me of my mother
生前在菜园里忙碌	who, while alive, busied herself in the vegetable garden
表情僵硬，唯有看我吃饭时	her face stiff, and only when I ate my meals
她的表情才会松弛	softened her smile
尽管我埋着头，尽管	though my head was bent, though
她不知道“茄子”的发音	she did not know the sound effect of eggplant
——这么神奇	—How miraculous
这么多年过去了	So many years have passed
我仍然能在每一张合影照中见到她	I still see in every picture we took together her
和她希望我成为的样子	and me with the look she wanted me to have

暮色中

我父亲在暮色中走来走去
他总是最后一个走进家门的人
除了背影，我几乎认不出他
当他日益佝偻，一大早
就坐在屋檐下等候天黑
我更加认不出他了
有时我也拉一张板凳在他对面坐下
仔细看他像一个孩子
讪笑着
粗糙的手掌搭在膝盖上
仿佛被人推进了照相馆
有些委屈，不好意思

AT TWILIGHT

My father walked about at twilight
always the last one to enter the house
Except for his back, I could hardly recognize him
When he got more stooped, early in the morning
he would sit under the eaves for the night to fall
It was then even harder to recognize him
Sometimes I'd sit on a stool, facing him
scrutinizing him as he like a child
forced a smile
rough hands on his lap
as if he had been pushed into a photo studio
a little wronged, and shy

草木灰

WOOD ASH

草木在灰中的样子	How plants look in ash
火焰最清楚	the blaze knows the best
我见过火焰	I know a blaze
用吹筒和火钳为它造过型	having shaped one with a blow tube and tongs
烟囱里的烟雾停留在几十年前	The smoke in the chimney stayed as it had been decades ago
几十年后我顺着烟道	Decades later following the pipe I
重新回到了这堆灰烬边	returned to the pile of ash
把烤过的红薯、鸡蛋和乌龟	Sweet potatoes, eggs, and turtles
重新翻烤了一遍	each I flipped over and baked again
屋后的山坡上草木连着草木	Behind the cottage up on the slope was vast vegetation
原有的小径已然消逝	while the original little path was traceless
我先在雨中埋葬了母亲	I buried first my mother in the rain
随后又在雪中埋葬了父亲	and then my father, under the snow

奔丧之路　　ON THE WAY TO FUNERALS

绿皮火车在冰天雪地里走走停停
刺目的不仅仅是窗外的雪景
还有沿途墓碑似的站牌
我曾无数次走在这条路上
现在才意识到
省亲之路也是奔丧之路
而我其实是那个隐形的筑路工
一边起早贪黑地修路
一边胆战心惊地冀望着
此路不通，至少越晚越好

The green train ran stop-and-go on ice and snow
What's glaring was not just snow outside the window
but also stop signs that looked like tombstones along the way
I had travelled on this road numerous times
But only now did I realize
visiting my loved ones was also returning home for their funerals
and I was really that invisible railroad builder
laboring all day on building the road
and horrified by the wish that
the road would stay incomplete, or at least as delayed as possible

祭父诗

一般来说，树有多高
它的根须就有多长
有时候你无法想象
落日在离开你之后变成了
谁脸上的朝阳
地平线由远及近
黑暗中的事物越复杂越集中
父亲挖的树蔸歪靠在树坑旁
斩断的根须仍然在抽搐

IN MEMORY OF MY FATHER

Generally speaking, the height of a tree
is proportional to the length of its roots
Sometimes it's hard to imagine
after the sun sets for you
to whom has it risen
The horizon approaches from afar
in the dark, the more complicated appears the more
concentrated
The stump my father dug up lay slanted near the hole
the chopped roots still convulsing

每家都有上山的人

EVERY FAMILY HAS SOMEONE WHO RESTS ON THAT MOUNTAIN

父亲搬进了新居
清明那天
房前屋后涌来了很多人
都在外面站着
烧纸，焚香，放鞭，磕头
冷风吹着呼呼作响的雨披
也将燃尽的纸屑吹向了
阴云密布的天空
没有人知道我的父亲是谁
我的兄弟们也不知道
当我跪在他新居门前
我能从虚掩的门缝里看见
他生前的老样子——
他坐在半山腰的公路旁
望着一辆辆汽车从山脚下驶来
在路边停下，然后绝尘而去
尘土依旧在飞扬
没有人知道尘世的真正模样

My father moved to his new home
On the Tomb Sweeping Day
people flocked to us from all directions
In the open air
they left offerings, burnt joss sticks, set off
firecrackers, and bowed
while cold wind whirled against their raincoats
and blew the burned paper into
the overcast sky
Nobody knew what my father was
not even my brothers did
When I knelt in front of his new home
from the unlatched opening I could see
the old look of him—
He sat by a road halfway up the mountain
looking at cars from the foot of the mountain
stop by, and stir up and leave a dust cloud
Dust still swirls in the air
and nobody knows the real look of this world

姐姐

我二姐曾经给我做过一双鞋垫
纯棉的，手工的，绣花的
上面绣着：一路平安
这是在二十多年前，我的脚
已经停止生长
我穿上它走了很多年
鞋子换了数双
鞋垫也早已磨穿
我记得最后一次见到它
是在去喀纳斯的路上
坐在白哈巴的一座山顶
我一边看晚霞
一边脱下鞋子磕着沙子
鞋垫掉了出来，但只是
几块彩色的布片
这件事我从来没有对人讲过
有时我在路上走
总感觉有人在身后叫我
手里也举着这样一双鞋垫
也像当年二姐那样
站在每一条道路的起点

SISTER

My second older sister once made me a pair of shoe insoles
cotton, handcrafted, embroidered
with the message: Bon Voyage
That was more than two decades ago, when my feet
had already stopped growing
I wore the pair for years
with shoes replaced many times
and the insoles long worn out
I remember the last time I saw the insoles was
on the way to Kanas
Sitting on a summit at Baihaba
while enjoying the sunset
I took off my shoes to shake out sand
when the insoles fell out; they were merely
a few colored cloth fragments
I have never revealed to anyone
that sometimes when I walk
I always feel like somebody is calling me from behind
with a similar pair of insoles in hand
exactly like my sister once did
at the start of each road

作物的秘密

白菜的邻居永远是萝卜
青椒的周围是苦瓜和豇豆
丝瓜走亲戚路上会遇到葫芦
我兄弟领着我
一会儿像地主
一会儿像奴仆
松树看见他拎了把斧头
荆条看见我拿了把镰刀

SECRET OF CROPS

Cabbages take turnips as their forever companions
Green peppers are surrounded by bitter melons and cowpeas
Luffas meet gourds on the way to visit relatives
My big brother led me
sometimes like a landlord
other times like a servant
Pine trees saw him carrying an axe
and twigs of chaste trees saw me holding a sickle

风吹树叶的声音

SOUND OF WIND BLOWING LEAVES

不进我屋子的风只是风声
如果没有树
它路过的时候可能无声无息
现在它抱着一棵樟树摇来晃去
让两片老死不相往来的树叶
终于有机会贴在了一起
像两个孪生兄弟
一出生就各自东西
我站在风的外面打量它们
我站在窗前倾听风声
我的头顶上是一台木质吊扇
整个夏天它都在转啊转
如果它停止转动了
就意味着我出门
去找我的孪生兄弟去了

Wind that does not enter my room is merely sound
If not for the trees
it would be silent as it passes
Now it holds a camphor tree and swirls about it
enabling two isolated leaves
to finally have the chance to stick together
like twin brothers
who headed out on separate ways since birth
I stand outside the wind to observe the leaves
I stand by the window to listen to the sound of wind
Over my head a wood ceiling fan
has been spinning all summer
If it stops
it means I have gone
to find my twin brother

交谈

天空和大地通过雨水来交谈
说情话时下毛毛雨
吵架时用暴雨和雷电
疾风中的山与山
树与树
前者孤傲
后者点头哈腰
它们都用风声来交谈
微风拂过沧桑的脸
狂风再用力抽打一遍
多年未见的亲人
隔着越来越紧张的土壤
交谈，用最诚实的方言
他低声说想她
又高声说了一遍
当他哭泣时眼泪是最好的
谈资，再紧张的土壤
也有松动之时

TALK

The sky and land talk through rain
they speak of love with a drizzle
and they fight like a storm with thunder and lightning
In a blast of mountains
or trees
the former remains aloof
the latter bows and scrapes
They all talk in the sound of wind
the breeze brushes over the weather-beaten face
and howling wind adds with another strike
They who haven't seen each other for years
across ever hard-pressed soil will
talk; in a most honest dialect
he murmurs his longing for her
and then announces it loudly
When he cries, his tears make for
the best talk; even the hardest pressed soil
can loosen up sometimes

在一起

1986 年我的父亲母亲在黄鹤楼
留下过一张合影。没想到，
这成了他俩现存的唯一的
一张合影照
母亲去世后，父亲把它翻出来
父亲去世后，我们把它翻出来
打算用在他们的合墓碑上
从去年清明节开始计划这件事
但按老家的规矩
得在三年之后才能落实
现在每次回去我都要
先去母亲的坟前劝她再耐心点
再去父亲的墓前劝他不要着急
现在每次看到这张合影
都感觉有一把看不见的尺子
在丈量着他俩生前的距离
死后的距离，以及
他们与我之间的距离
在一起的愿望从来不曾这样强烈

TOGETHER

In 1986 at the Yellow Crane Tower my father and mother
took a photo. Hard to imagine
this turns out to be the only existing photo
of them together
After my mother passed away, my father dug it out
After my father passed away, we dug it out
intending to put it up on the tombstone for both of them
We set about the ritual from last Tomb-Sweeping Day
but according to the hometown tradition
the whole process would not end until three years later
Now each time I go back to visit my hometown
I persuade my mother, in front of her tomb, to be patient
Then I ask my father, in front of his tomb, not to worry
Every time I examine the photo
I feel an invisible ruler
measuring the distance between them in life
after their passing, and
between them and me
The desire to be together has never been so intense

为罗平油菜花而作

FOR CANOLA FLOWERS IN LUOPING

床单铺好了就应该睡觉
春困的人在罗平
却怎么也睡不着
蜜蜂在侧，春光大泄
磨油坊里的灯火从古至今
一直在跳跃
死去的父亲蹲在床头
抽烟，咳嗽
死去的母亲一次次
将四散的菜籽归拢
那些孤儿一般黝黑的菜籽
从命运的指缝间滑落
我是其中滚得最远的那一颗
独自灿烂，独自落寞

Bed ready, I should be sleeping
But spring fatigue in Luoping
made me sleepless
Bees humming, light bright
the oil lamp in the mill since ancient time
has been flickering
I see my deceased father crouching on the bed
smoking, coughing
my deceased mother again and again
trying to bring the scattered seeds together
Like orphans, the dark oil seeds
gradually fell through fate's fingertips
and I was the one that fell the farthest
blooming alone, gloomy alone

给花旦找墓地

FINDING THE RESTING PLACE FOR HUA DAN

这是一首迟到的诗
一首想写却迟迟不敢动笔的诗
这是一首早有预谋的诗
我预料过你的死但没有料到
你死后这么久还栩栩如生
枇杷树没有结枇杷
你躺在树下
这是一首强忍着泪水的诗
直到临死你水汪汪的眼睛
还在看我，还在看我
怎样把没有你的日子过到底

This is a belated poem
one intended but delayed by hesitation
This is a premeditated poem
I had anticipated your passing but I had not expected
you to look so vivid after it
There are no fruits on the loquat tree
where you lie in eternal peace
This is a poem that holds back tears
Until the last moment your watery eyes
were still watching me, watching
how I would live without you

大雪进山

太雪是晚上来的
早上还没有离开的意思
第二天上午父亲叫上我
跟他一起进山走亲戚
根本就没有路可走
但父亲在前面走着
我跟着他，从一个清晰的
脚窝挪到另一个模糊的脚窝
雪越下越大
昨天还见过的山已经不见了
父亲领着我往雪堆上走
父亲带着我在雪堆里穿梭
直到一股浓烟将我们拦下
那是我见过的
最黑的烟囱
发黄的炊烟紧贴着屋檐
陈旧的亲戚站在屋檐下
呵出的热气模糊了他
乐呵呵的脸

SNOW IN THE MOUNTAINS

Snow started during the night
and refused to let up even into the next day
My father summoned me up in the morning
to visit with him a relative in the mountains
There was literally no road to walk on
but my father plunged ahead
I followed, moving from one distinctive
footprint to a blurry one
Snow fell heavier and heavier
Yesterday's mountains disappeared from view
My father led me towards the snow banks
and we wove in and out of the snow piles
until we were stopped by a thick smoke
as far as I knew
the darkest of its kind
The yellowish smoke stayed close to the roof of a house
and our old relative stood under the roof
hot air from his breathing blurring
his cheerful face

最遥远的雪

想起雪后的那些晚上
天空清凉，还有星星
我能看到你家的屋顶
以及屋后黛色的竹林
半夜里旷野上传来
树枝脆断的声响
有人踏雪归来，含着痰
想起我们在一起的日子
阳光刺眼，看不清
雪人明晃晃的表情
只有胡萝卜是橙黄的
只有桃核做的眼睛圆睁着
我们走在结了冰的塘面上
身前身后都是冰面的炸裂声
想起你至今没有上岸
最后的雪积在人去屋空的檐下
每天静静地化一点
我忍不住朝天边探了探身体

THE FARTHEST SNOW

I am recollecting those nights after the snow
the sky was clear and cool, and star-dotted
I could see the roof of your family's house
and the dark bamboo grove behind it
At midnight from the open fields
came snapping sounds of tree branches
someone returned from the snow, phlegm in the throat
I am reminiscing about those days we shared
The sun was glaring, blinding us from
the bright expression of the snowman
other than the carrot yellow
other than the round wide-open eyes made of walnuts
We walked on the frozen pond
ice crackling before and behind us
I am thinking of you still not ashore
The last snow piled under the eaves of your empty house
melting quietly each day, bit by bit
I cannot but lean towards the faraway firmament

我的梦

MY DREAMS

我发现我的梦
总在同一座房子里面发生
那是我年幼时生活过的地方
父母健在，姊妹参差不齐
我在这座房子里梦见过
许多从来没有到过这里的人
我和你一起把钓回来的鱼
开肠剖肚，我和你一起
把生米煮熟
把不可能发生的事一一经历
而这究竟是怎么回事
我发现我的梦一旦回到这里
就顺理成章了，无人打搅
仿佛记忆里最遥远的那部分
在苏醒。老房子依然明亮
午后的阳光照着土黄的墙壁
我靠在微微发烫的墙面上
天空蔚蓝，仔细看
星光遥远犹如胃中的米粒

I find my dreams
always take place in the same house
That's where I spent my childhood
my parents alive, my sisters different from each other
I dreamed in that house
of many who had never been there
You and I took the fish we had caught
and gutted it; you and I
"cooked the raw rice"
doing all the impossible one thing at a time
Why is it
I find my dreams once returned to the house
all become logical, undisturbed
as if the remotest story woke
from memory. The old house was still bright
as the afternoon sun shone on its yellow ochre wall
I leaned against the slightly hot surface
the sky azure, and scrutinized
the stars as remote as the rice grains in a stomach

容我喝口井水

从水缸到水井的距离
从前很远，现在更遥远了
挑水的人走在记忆中
像田埂游弋在茂盛的草丛里
我听见木瓢磕碰桶沿的声音
清冽又甜美
也能看见虫豸在黄昏
从这里飞向那里
但我已经无法指认水井的位置
方位肯定是对的
但那是月亮升起的方向
挑水的人走在月光下
换肩的时候他与月亮对视
而另一轮明月正在天井角落的
水缸里等候他
像一只白瓷碗
反扣在没有桌面的桌子上

ALLOW ME TO TAKE A SIP OF THE WELL WATER

From the water vat to the well
used to be very far, but now it is even farther
He who carried water walks in my memory
like field ridges meandering in lush grass
I hear the wood scoop knocking against his bucket's side
its sound, cool, clear and sweet
Insects are also visible
flying here and there
but I cannot pinpoint the position of the well
The direction must be right
but the well was where the moon rose
the water carrier walked in moonlight and
exchanged looks with the moon as he switched the load from
one shoulder to the other
while all the time in the corner of the courtyard another
bright moon was
waiting for him in the vat
very much like a white porcelain bowl
lying upside down on the surfaceless table

一把米

脱粒机和风斗
是怎么做到的
两升谷
一斗米
是怎么做到的
推磨的人说磨盘太小了
喂谷的人抱怨谷子硌手
我在一事无成的年纪
手握一把米
学着喂磨
我学会的歌
他们早就不再唱和

A FISTFUL OF RICE

How could the threshing and winnowing machines
make certain
two kilograms of grains became
one bucket of rice
How could it be possible
one person complained of quern-stones being too small
and the other of hands hurt due to feeding grains into mach
At the age of being nothing
grains in hand, I
learned to feed grains
Songs I learned
they stopped responding to a long time ago

在桃林

AT THE PEACH ORCHARD

桃花离开后，来了
一些桃子在树叶的掩护下
她们慢慢发育
朝阳的山坡
风吹水皱
小学的高音喇叭在做完体操后
终于放低了嗓门
我见过越来越多的陌生人
从山下上来了就不想下去
因为这片桃林他们幻想过
同气连枝的生活

After peach blossoms came
peaches covered by leaves
slowly ripened
Against the sunny slope
water rippled as breeze blew
After morning exercise the elementary school's loudspeaker
finally lowered its blast
I saw more and more strangers
moved up to the hills and stayed
Because of the orchard they fancied
a life of the same breath and branches

交换

拿一枚鸡蛋去交换一枚鸭蛋
哪一个更划算?
拿一枚刚刚从自家鸡窝里捡拾的鸡蛋
去七月的岩子河边
找牧鸭女交换一枚鸭蛋
哪一个更划算?
鸡蛋小而鸭蛋大
鸡蛋少而鸭蛋多
哪一个更划算?
我站在七月的岩子河边，远远
望着溯流而上的鸭群
鸭毛漫天飞舞
牧鸭女身后拖拽着一根竹竿
我一遍一遍地摩挲着口袋里的鸡蛋
想象着搁浅在河床上的鸭蛋
许多年过去了我还记得
那位从下游来的女孩
蓬松而卷曲的头发
被阳光烫伤了的鸭蛋型的脸

EXCHANGES

A chicken egg bartering for a duck egg
which gets a better deal?
Take a chicken egg fresh from your own chicken coop
and go to the Yanzi River in July
to barter for a duck egg from the duck farm girl
who gets a better deal?
Chicken eggs are small while duck eggs are big
The number of chicken eggs is smaller than that of the ducks
which is a better deal?
In July I stood by the Yanzi River, watching from afar
a paddling of ducks floating upstream
duck feathers dancing in the air
The farm girl dragged along a bamboo pole
I kept rubbing the chicken egg in my pocket
thinking of the duck egg stranded in the riverbed
After many years I still remember
that girl from the lower reaches of the river
her fluffy and curly hair
her sunburnt egg-shaped face

替我回家的人

HE WHO RETURNED HOME FOR ME

替我回家的人给我带回来
三样东西——
松香、桃胶和地衣
每一样都酷似我记忆中的样子
每一样都有出处和来历——
松香照见了黑松林里的
那座几乎平塌的孤坟
桃胶透亮，像一簇挣扎着
从桃树内部挤出来的光
我记得最可口的扁桃
长在活死人门前的堰堤上
夏夜里，他就睡在树下
楠竹凉床吱吱作响
而一场雨后，被践踏过的
青草翻山越岭来到了
我即将离开的故土
大地空濛，蹲踞其上的
是深秋的草木
从天末吹过来的凉风
让捡地衣的母亲想到了我
她抬头望望飞奔的云朵
她低头加快了手中的动作

He who returned home for me brought back
three things—
rosin, peach gum, and lichen
each matching perfectly my memory of them
each having their own origin and history—
Rosin lit up the dark pine forest
illuminating the almost flat lonely tomb
Peach gum was translucent, like struggling
light oozing out of peach trees
The most delectable peach gum I remember
grew on the weir in front of the village slob's door
In summer, he would lie asleep under the tree
his bamboo lounger squeaking
After rain, the once trodden grass
would re-carpet the hill and dale of
the hometown I would soon leave
Crouched on the vast hazy land
was deep autumn vegetation
Cool wind blowing at the end of day
reminded my lichen-gathering mother of me
She looked up and saw clouds traveling fast
She lowered her head and quickened the hands

春日望乡

HOMEWARD THOUGHTS ON A SPRING DAY

犁耙水响的时节
你回了一趟老家
插秧人正把一整块拥挤的绿
均匀地分撒
在荡漾的泥水中
一行一行的绿
从这头看过去是青翠
从那头看过来是葱郁
田埂上，犁尖闪亮
槐花树下缠绕着长长的牛绳
你沿着田埂走来走去
你走过那么多的路
却没有哪一条路像田埂这样
让你走着走着就感觉到
已经回家了
却怎么也找不到家门

During the plowing and harrowing season
you went back to your hometown
The villagers were transplanting packed green seedlings
into even chunks
In the rippling muddy waters
lines of green
looked verdant from this end
and lush from the other
On a field ridge, a plow's blade shone brightly
and a long cow rope twined around the sophora tree
You walked around along the ridges
You had walked on many roads
but none like the field ridges
made you feel that step by step
you had reached home
yet could not find its gate

我还是喜欢你明亮的样子

I STILL LIKE THE DAZZLING YOU

我还是喜欢你明亮的样子
你在子宫里的样子
我还是喜欢你母亲孕育你的
样子，人群闪避，草坡平缓
的样子；我还是喜欢她
恋爱的样子
背转身去接电话
拆信时迫不及待的样子
我还是喜欢
那样，那时候
空气天真，你无所不能

I still like the dazzling you
in the womb
I still like the look of your mother carrying you
crowds yielding and grassy slope gentle
I still like her look of
a woman-in-love
turning back to answer the phone
or unable to refrain from opening a letter
I still like
that; that time
the air was innocent and you, omnipotent

从音乐学院到实验中学

从音乐学院到实验中学
昨天我走了三千零六十八步
一千步是彭刘杨邮局
两千步是司门口天桥
三千步是中百仓储
我记下它们，以便
替今天作这样的辩护：
“哦，这不是重复，是必需！”
而今天，我还会这样走——
五点钟下楼
五点零五分是实验小学
五点十分是工商银行大楼
五点二十分是户部巷口
五点三十三分我加入攒动的人头
在千百件校服中间
搜寻这只饭盒的主人
我还会捂着温热的盒底
像一个托钵僧
站在梧桐树下，夕光越过树梢
俗世潦草，所谓幸福
就是用手去触摸一个人的额头

FROM THE CONSERVATORY TO THE EXPERIMENTAL MIDDLE SCHOOL

From the Conservatory to the School
yesterday it took me three thousand and sixty-
eight steps
One thousand steps to the Peng-Liu-Yang Post
Office
Two thousand steps to Simenkou Overpass
Three thousand steps to Zhongbai Warehouse
I recorded them, to
defend today in such logic:
Oh, no. It's not repetition; it's necessity!
And today, I would still walk this way—
Leave the building at five
reach the School at 5:05
reach the ICBC building at 5:10
reach Hubu Alley at 5:20
and then join the moving crowd of people at 5:33
and locate among hundreds of uniformed
students
the owner of this lunchbox
I would still hold the bottom of the box
like a dervish
standing under the sycamore, with sunset light
passing the treetops
Unpolished, the so-called happiness of this
secular world is
merely touching the forehead of a person
with a hand

狗年忆狗

墙壁转角处
满是花旦的蹭痕
昨天做卫生
我对我说：
再也不养宠物了
话音刚落就看见花旦
在照片里
怔怔地望着我
那无辜的神情
栩栩如生
如同它在世时
每次我们出门
从门缝里钻出的
那最后一瞥——
门关上
它趴下
侧耳倾听
熟悉的足音
与陌生的世界汇合
它只能无力地
从一个墙角踱到另一个墙角
它不记得自己在我们不在的
时候干过什么
现在我替它记下了
那长达数年的惯性
再用一块抹布轻轻拭去

REMEMBERING MY DOG IN THE YEAR OF THE DOG

The corner of the walls
teems with scuff marks left by Hua Dan
Yesterday while doing cleaning
I told myself:
Do not keep pets anymore
Before my voice faded away I saw Hua Dan
in the photo
staring at me
That innocent look
so lifelike
resembled what she did
each time my family headed out
from the crack of the door
she would give us a last look—
The door closed
and she would lie on her stomach
listening attentively
to the familiar footfall
merging with the strange world
Left with no means she could only
pace from one corner to another
unable to remember during our absence
what she did
I am recording on her behalf
those years of momentum
before gently wiping away the marks with a
cloth

深筒胶鞋

我穿着深筒胶鞋一步路也走不动
我的下半身陷进了鞋筒
我不清楚父亲是怎样做到的
整个雨季他就住在鞋筒里
这是多么神奇的事情
他迈开大步，神气活现地
走在雨中
走进水坑里
我在午夜听见胶鞋进门的声音
咣当咣当的声音
从一间屋漫进另一间屋
我从来没有留意过父亲的脚
早上醒来，我看见那双鞋
倒扣在台阶上
在阳光里冒着热气
我试着用手去探测鞋筒的深度
我把两只手臂都留在了潮湿阴暗的地方
那里有他脚趾抠出的浅窝
太阳爬上了屋脊
不久以后阳光消逝
父亲赤脚走在软和的泥地上
我还是没有看清他的脚
但他的脚印到处都有

HIGH RUBBER RAINBOOTS

I could barely move in knee-high rubber
    rainboots
my lower body deeply buried in those shoes
I couldn't figure out how Dad did it
the whole rainy season he might well have lived
    in his boots
How miraculous that
he could take high-spirited strides
in rain
through puddles
At midnight I heard rubber boots stepping into
    the door
thumping, thumping
from one room to another
though I had never paid attention to Dad's feet
When awoke in the morning, I saw his boots
laying upside down on the steps
steaming in sunlight
I tried to measure the height of the shoes
only to find both arms reached dark and damp
    places
with light holes dug by his toes
The sun climbed onto the roof peak
before it soon disappeared
Dad walked barefoot on the soft soil
I still did not see clearly his feet
but his footprints were everywhere

停止生长的脚

我穿 41 码的鞋子
40 码找过我
42 码找不到我
我穿我妻子给我买的鞋子
好像只有她知道
什么样式适合我的脚
我穿皮鞋，运动鞋
几乎从不穿凉鞋
走在你也走过的路上
只有当我赤脚时
我走的路才是我自己的路
我不穿鞋的时候我的脚
在回望那条路
我不穿鞋的时候那条路上
有我深深浅浅的脚模
我的拇指总爱那样翘着
当它往下抠时
我一定正陷在泥泞中
我已经很多年没有赤脚走路了
我最后一次在岩子河里洗脚
是在哪一年的隆冬？
那一年我的脚已经停止了生长
我母亲还活着
我记得她把我的鞋样夹在了
一摞废弃的高考复习资料中
此后只有指甲在生长
只有鞋子在重复着脚的形状

FEET THAT STOPPED GROWING

I wear size 41 shoes
size 40 once worked for me
but size 42 has never been a fit
I wear shoes purchased by my wife
who seems the only one who knows
the right style of shoes for me
I wear leather shoes and sneakers
barely any sandals
and walk on the road everyone walks on
Only when I walk barefoot
does a road become my own
When shoeless, my feet
would look backwards
and see the road I took
full of deep or shallow imprints
My big toe liked to point up
when it pointed down
I must have been stranded in mud
I have not walked barefoot for many years
When was the last midwinter
I soaked my feet in the Yanzi River?
That year my feet had stopped growing
and my mother was still alive
I remember she had sandwiched my shoe pattern
in a pile of abandoned study materials for the
    college exam
After that only my toenails continued to grow
only my shoes duplicated my feet's shape

在烈日下想象 一场暴雨

我父亲蹲在烟叶地里想象着
一场雨，最好是一场暴雨
我的母亲坐在槐树下剥豆子
每剥几个豆荚就朝池塘方向望一下
我的两个姐姐正手持钩镰
一个在采莲花，一个在摘莲蓬
我哥哥正在柳树下擦拭
公家的手扶拖拉机
我见他拿起摇把，又放下摇把
我的狗，两条狗都趴在屋檐下
我的鸡，一群鸡都在竹园里打盹
穿堂风穿过凉席的时候
我正要瞌睡，门前晾衣绳上
的衣裤突然活蹦乱跳起来
乌云从西南角飞奔而至
乌云之下传来敲锣打鼓的声音
有几滴鼓点落在了我身边
那只倒扣着的洋瓷盆底

IMAGINE A HEAVY RAINFALL IN THE SCORCHING SUN

Dad was squatting in the tobacco field imagining
a rainfall, better yet, a heavy one
Mom was peeling beans under the locust tree
every so often she'd look up in the direction of the
pond
My two sisters were each holding a sickle
one collecting lotus flowers and the other, lotus
heads
Under the willow tree my big brother was
polishing
the village's hand tractor
I saw him pulling up the crank and then letting
it down
My dogs, two, curled up under the roof
My chickens, a flock, were dozing off in the
bamboo grove
When a draught of air passed through my
sleeping matt
I was about to sleep; then on the front yard
clothesline
garments suddenly started to blow about lively
Dark clouds closed in from the southwest
Underneath them came the sounds of drums
and gongs
and beside me a few drops beat onto
that enamel basin laid bottom up

拉链与纽扣

大雁像一排拉链
从最美的天空飞过
最美的脖颈、肩胛
令人眩晕
我在想象中见过它们
日落时分的河滩上
几只掉队的野鸭惊呼着
重新返回空中
像几枚纽扣。我见过
你在黑夜里冰凉的手
我见过你哆嗦着解开
又在慌乱中系紧的
那颗暗红的水晶纽扣
在最好的年纪
它的坚定与踌躇

ZIPPER AND BUTTON

Like a zipper the wild geese
flew across the most beautiful sky
their most appealing neck and shoulder
so stunning
I have imagined them in my mind
Sundown on the beach
a few of them, falling behind, shouting
to return to the sky
like a few buttons. I saw
your cold hand in dark nights
I saw your trembling hand unbuttoned
and then flustered to refasten
that deep red crystal button
at the sweetest age
with determination and hesitation

篇六 燕燕于飞，下上其音

VI. *Oh swallows, sing in varied note/to each other for sweet succor.*

雪后三天

雪后三天还没有化完
太阳红着脸出现
在乱蓬蓬的地平线
公路两端，水牛和卡车相向
而行，它们将在桥头碰面
结过冰的河早晚都很平静
小儿摸着桥墩上的狮子头
老汉弯腰拔扯亡妻的坟上草
残雪不多不少
正好映亮了屋顶
东边的炊烟升起来了
西边的炊烟在竹林里缠绕
一条狗站在路中间
侧耳听辨碗筷的声音

THREE DAYS AFTER THE SNOW

After three days some snow remains unmelted
The sun has risen red faced
on the untidy horizon
On the road a buffalo and a truck are heading
towards each other; they will meet at the bridge
The frozen river appears quiet both morning and evening
A little child is touching the head of the bridge's stone lion
while an old man is bending down to pull weeds by his wife's
tomb
The right amount of lingering snow
has brightened the roofs
Cooking smoke is rising from the east
and from the west swirling around the bamboo grove
Standing in the middle of the road a dog
is turning his ears to tell the sounds of bowls and chopsticks

星期天的雪

SUNDAY SNOW

星期天的雪
星期一化一点
星期二化一点
到了星期三还没有化完
太阳出来了
照着星期四的屋顶
月亮出来了
挂在星期五的山头
星期六一整天都在泥泞中
傍晚红霞满天
半夜树枝折断
星期天的早晨大雪覆满门径
人世安静莫过于雪落无声
你在天光下沉睡
你梦见了给你温暖的人

Sunday snow
melted a bit on Monday
melted more on Tuesday
but some of it remained unmelted by Wednesday
The sun rose
shining on the Thursday roof
The moon appeared
hanging over the mountain of Friday
The whole Saturday was muddy
yet at sunset the sky turned all crimson
and a branch broke amid the night
On Sunday morning heavy snow fully covered the doorway
The world couldn't be quieter than the silent snowfall
You slept deeply in daylight
and dreamed of the one who gave you warmth

冬日速写

SKETCH OF A WINTER DAY

麦地尽头是一块菜地
菜地过去是一座池塘
池塘上方又是一块麦地
走过麦地是一座橘园
橘子树上有几颗橘子
橘园下面有一片竹林
竹林深处是一户人家
家里的人都出门去了
门前的柳树和槐树在落叶
树杈举着比树干更黑的鸟巢
黑白相间的喜鹊在更高的枝丫上叫

At the end of the wheat field is a vegetable field
beyond which is a pond
that borders another wheat field on the far end
Passing that wheat field you reach an orchard
in which a few oranges hang on the citrus trees
Next to the orchard is a bamboo grove
deep into which is the homestead of a family
who are not at home for the moment
In the front yard leaves are falling from the willow and locust trees
whose branches hold bird nests darker than the tree bark
on whose even higher twigs black and white magpies are chirping

彩虹出现的时候　WHEN THE RAINBOW APPEARS

松树洗过之后松针是明亮的	Pine needles shone after rain washed pine trees
河流浑浊，像一截短裤	The river was turbid, like a pair of muddy pants
路在翻山	The road climbed over the mountain
而山在爬坡	and the mountain was climbing a steep slope
画眉在沟渠边鸣叫	A thrush was chirping in a field-edge ditch
卷尾鸟在电线杆上应和	echoed by a drongo on a power line
松树林的这边是松树	Beyond this side of the pine trees were more pine trees
松树林的那边除了松树	Beyond that side of the pine trees were more pine trees
还有一群站在弧光里的人	along with a crowd of people standing under the rainbow arc
他们仰着头	They leaned back their heads
他们身后的牲畜也仰着头	and behind them their livestock followed suit

旧时光

OLD DAYS

埋头吃草的牛
吃着吃着就翻过了
半阴半阳的山坡
最后一眼看它的人
也消逝在了芝麻地尽头
玩弹珠的孩子弹珠一样
蹦跳在彩色的山坳间
黄昏已然降临
远去的牛铃声在远去
远去的呼唤声
却越来越清晰

Head bent the cow grazed on grass
While it grazed it also went around
the half-shaded slope
The last person who saw it
also disappeared into the sesame fields
Like the marbles they played with, children
scampered around in the colorful valley
Dusk already fell
The cowbell chimed and faded far away
yet the distant calls
became clearer and clearer

春分十三行

我和我的老狗并排走
在正午的风中
像去年的这个时候
像昨天的这个时候
我们一前一后走在风中
像畜生一样走着
像人类一样走着
空洞的头顶上
去年的叶子在风中落下
今年的叶子在风中生长
我和我的老狗一直会走到墙根下
它撒尿的时候
我望着正在爬墙的茑萝

THIRTEEN LINES FOR SPRING EQUINOX

I walk side by side with my old dog
against the wind of high noon
like we did the same time last equinox
like we did the same time yesterday
We walk one after the other in the wind
like beasts do
like human beings do
Overhead in the hollow sky
leaves of last year are falling in the wind
and leaves of this year are growing in the wind
My dog and I will walk all the way to the foot of the wall
When she pees
I will be examining the creeping cypress vines

树上的爱情

桃子看着桃子
看着桃子
那么远那么近
一天又一天
因为相爱而相似
桃子看着桃子
脸红了
羞答答的
垂下眼睑
稍一分神就落了下来
滚落在一起
桃子依然看着桃子
直到桃核裂开
他们的爱
因无人打搅而周而复始

LOVE ON THE TREE

One peach looks at another
looks at another
They are so far apart and yet so close
Day by day
their mutual love makes them look alike
One peach looks at another
blushing
bashful
they lower their eyes
Slightly distracted
they fall to the ground and roll to each other
One peach still looks at another
until the pit bursts
Their love
without disturbance perpetuates itself

仿《枕草子》

鸟鸣是春天的好听，尤其是
第二场春雨后
清晨，大多数人还在熟睡
你也在黑暗中
凭声音去猜测鸟的身份很有意思
彩鹬，鹊鹞，乌灰鸫，黄腰柳莺……
水杉高过了屋顶
水杉之上还有其他事物
若是从空中往下看
即便看不清，那些摇摆着的
嫩枝也一定有趣
那些还没有来得及掉落的叶子
哀求着的生命
是很有意味的

IN THE STYLE OF *THE PILLOW BOOK*

Birds chirp the best in spring, especially
after the second rain
In the morning, when most are still in deep sleep
and you in darkness as well
it is very interesting to identify the birds by their chirping
Painted-snipe, pied harrier, Japanese thrush, yellow-
rumped willow warbler…
The dawn redwood outgrows the roof
but above the tree there is yet something else
If viewed from the air
even though seen unclearly, those swaying
tender branches are still intriguing
and those leaves about to fall
like pleading lives
are very fascinating

无题

UNTITLED

花一样的蝴蝶落在了蝴蝶一样的花上
起风的时候，蝴蝶不动
风停了，蝴蝶煽动翅膀

The flower-like butterfly lands on a flower that
resembles a butterfly
When the wind blows, the butterfly stays motionless
When the wind lets up, the butterfly flaps its wings

无题

摸过的耳垂会记得你的手指
如果是在冰凉的冬日
摸过的手心里会印满燃烧的螺纹
人间辽阔而你涉世未深
一想到所见并非所有
而这就是生活，就有一阵风
从裤管里面钻过
就有一种愿望跋山涉水
在断头路上来回走

UNTITLED

Once touched, the earlobe will remember your fingers
If it were an ice-cold winter day
the palm of your hand would bear a burning imprint
of the earlobe
The world is vast while you are inexperienced
When you realize what you see is not what you have
and this is your life, you will feel a gust of wind
passing through your trousers
and a desire crossing mountains and rivers
to travel back and forth on the dead-end highways

无题

有些梦只能停留在梦中
既无兑现的可能
也无变成现实的必要
譬如你对我的好
止于我知道你是为了我好
反之亦然
反之这些梦
一如乱石堆满床头
你在乱坟岗上见过的星光
其实是这些梦的磷火

UNTITLED

Some dreams should stay in dreams
neither can they become true
nor is it necessary
such as your feelings toward me
should stop at my awareness of them
and vice versa
If not these dreams
will be like stones piled at bedside
and the starlight you see at the unmarked burial sites
are merely the will-o'-the-wisp of these dreams

无题

年纪大了梦想就会变小
当我意识到
某一天
我从大梦中醒来
脑海里却没有梦过的划痕
脸上也无悲无喜
当这一天无声无息地
来到我身边
像今天这样
蜷在床头
窗外，樟树叶正在经过隆冬
寒风熨着苍茫的人境
我几乎就要度过
这意犹未尽的一生

UNTITLED

The older we get the smaller our dreams become
If I realize
on a certain day
I wake up from my dream
yet there isn't any trace of a dream
nor expression of any kind on my face
If that day quietly
slips into my life
like what was today
me crouching at the bed
outside, leaves of the camphor tree trying to survive a cold
    winter
and wind chilling the vast human world
then I am almost done with
this tapering life

夜钓记

——给我的兄弟王琳，兼致方延伟

用电筒照射黑暗的河面
被照亮的那部分像
一张透光的宣纸
游到纸面上的草鱼
打了个旋
又游到了纸的背面
在涟漪中抖动浮标
在心情平静时想一想
激动人心的往事
想一想我们
在上游浪花里的那些日子
水在河里几乎没有费力
为什么却让人感觉筋疲力尽

NIGHT FISHING

—To My Brother Wang Lin, As Well As Fang Yanwei

Shine a flashlight onto the dark river surface
The lit part is like
a piece of transparent rice paper
The grass carp swims to the top of the paper
makes a turn
and then returns to the back
shaking the buoy in ripples
Ponder in a peaceful state of mind
over the exciting past
and contemplate why
in the days when we were swimming upstream
the water in the river was flowing effortlessly
but we felt exhausted

我的土豆树
——给易羊

每年春天我都会
把多余的土豆埋进花盆
自从我见过你的土豆树之后
自从你的树枯萎
每年的这个季节我都会
把剩下的当成是多余的
多余的生命又发了芽
多余的爱还在泥土下抓挠
死亡并不存在
如你所说
如我所愿
土豆树今天又长高了
土豆树明年还会继续长
我们坐在树下
谈一谈消逝
谈一谈久别重逢

MY POTATO "TREE"
—To My Friend Yi Yang

Every spring I would
bury left-over potatoes in a flower pot
Ever since I saw your potato "tree"
ever since it withered
each year at this season I would
treat the remainder as extra
Extra life sprouts
extra love reaches out under the soil
Death does not exist
as you said
as I wish
Now the tree has grown taller
and will continue to grow next year
Sitting under the tree we shall
talk about disappearance
talk about reunion after a long separation

地球上的地方
——给印

乘两班飞机再转
数小时的巴士
可以去任何地方
当我站在地球上打量
地球之外的任何地方
看见你正在转动
怀抱里的地球仪
你已经找到了自由
接下来你要寻找平静——
那么多的树木在森林中安息
你走在斑驳的林间
踩着阔叶林遇见了针叶林

PLACES ON EARTH
—To Yin

Two flights plus
a transfer to a bus ride of a few hours
can take one anywhere
When I stand on the earth and look around
what is beyond the earth
I see you turning
the globe in your arms
You have already found your freedom
and your next pursuit is tranquility—
So many trees rest in peace in the forest
In the dappled forests you walk
from the broadleaf to the coniferous

亲爱的弟弟

——致叶舟

从来就不存在穿肠而过的酒肉
所以你要在酒中歌唱
你的大漠、敦煌和黄河
从来都是花儿先开了
我们才会循着你的歌声去寻找
云在天上，天在河里
一个人活在另一个人的过去
从来都只有一个兰州
但每去一次就会多出一个来
像亲爱的弟弟
身边总多出一只酒杯
为他亲爱的祖国留着

DEAR LITTLE BROTHER

—To Ye Zhou

There has never been meat eating that does not bear karmic reaction
That's why, while drinking, you will sing
your desert, Dunhuang, and the Yellow River
It has always been after flowers bloom
that we follow your song to search for them
Clouds are in the sky, but the sky is in river water
One person always lives in the past of another
There has always been just one Lanzhou
but each time we go there another one comes into being
like a dear little brother
who always keeps an extra drinking glass
for his dear motherland

答枕边人，兼致新年

IN RESPONSE TO MY LOVE, TO THE NEW YEAR AS WELL

唯一的奇迹是身逢盛世
尚能恪守乱世之心
唯一的奖赏是
你还能出现在我的梦中
尽管是旧梦重温
长夜漫漫，肉体积攒的温暖
在不经意间传递
唯一的遗憾是，再也不能像恋人
那样盲目而混乱地生活
只能屈从于命运的蛮力
各自撕扯自己
再将这些生活的碎片拼凑成
一床百纳被
唯一的安慰是我们
并非天天活在雾霾中
太阳总会出来
像久别重逢的孩子
而我们被时光易容过的脸
变化再大，依然保留了
羞怯，和怜惜

The only miracle is to come upon the golden age
and yet still abide by the intent of the troubled times
The only reward is
you can still appcar in my dream
though it is an old one relived
in the long night, the bodily warmth absorbed
passing on unwittingly
The only regret is no longer able, like a lover, to
live blindly and aimlessly
Succumbed to the brute force of fate
torn apart by self-struggling
I sew scraps of life into
a patchwork quilt
The only consolation is that we
don't necessarily live in smog every day
The sun will rise
like the return of a child after a long separation
Our face much transformed by time
no matter how drastic the changes, maintains
its shininess, and tenderness

催咚催

CUI DONG CUI, IN THE STYLE OF A HUBEI FOLK SONG

打过菜籽的梿枷又打在了麦穗上	The flail for threshing rapeseeds is loosening wheat grains
捅过猪的刀早晚会捅进	The knife for butchering pigs sooner or later will thrust into
牛的喉咙——牛拉著石磙	the throat of the ox—which is still pulling the roller
一遍遍在禾场上走——	cycle after cycle on the threshing floor—
闪亮的刀尖必须用血蒙住	Shining blades must be covered by blood
而我们被尘埃蒙住了	while we must be shrouded in dust
快活的泥水从腮帮上滚下来	Muddy water drips merrily down from our cheeks
被大地稳稳接住	securely caught by the ground
死亡是一把巨大的扇子	Death is like a giant fan
扇得越快风却越小	the faster it moves the weaker the breeze
我蜷缩在星光下	I crouch under the starlight
听见扇子从你手上滑落	hearing the fan falling from your hand
看见又多活了一天的牛	and seeing the ox that gets to live another day
在黑暗中眨动着	batting in darkness its
妩媚的双眼皮和长睫毛	charming double-eyelid eyes and eyelashes

咏春调

TO THE TUNE OF SPRING

我母亲从来没有穿过花衣服
这是不是意味着
她从来就没有快乐过？
春天来了，但是最后一个春天
我背着她从医院回家
在屋后的小路上
她曾附在我耳边幽幽地说道：
“儿啊，我死后一定不让你梦到我
免得你害怕。我很知足，我幸福。”
十八年来，每当冬去春来
我都会想起那天下午
我背着不幸的母亲走
在开满鲜花的路上
一边走一边哭

My mother never wore bright colors
Does this mean
she had never been happy?
Spring came, the very last one
I carried her home from the hospital
On the road behind our house
she pressed against my ear and whispered:
“Sonny, after I'm gone, I will not allow you to dream of me
Don't want you to be afraid. I'm very content, and happy.”
Eighteen years now, at the turn from each winter to spring
I would recall that afternoon
My poor mother on my back
flowers blooming along the road
I wept while walking

有些花不开也罢

IT'S FINE IF SOME FLOWERS DO NOT BLOOM

"无花果的叶子就是无花果的花。"
——我忘了这是毛子还是东林说的
也忘了是在张家界还是涠洲岛
此刻我一边吃无花果一边上网查——
"无花果并非不开花，而是花小
藏于花托内，故又名隐花果……"
此刻，我似乎已经真理在握
却又感觉特别虚弱——因为
我也像一颗隐藏在花托中的果子
你们看到的我都是我的结果

"The leaves of the fig plant are its flowers."
—Can't remember if Maozi or Donglin said it
Nor was it in Zhangjiajie or on Weizhou Island
Now I am searching online as I eat figs—
"It's untrue that figs do not get flowers; their small flowers
are hidden in the receptacle, thus also known as a
syconium..."
Now, I seem to hold truth in my hand
but also feel extremely weak—because
like the flower hidden in a receptacle
what you see is merely the fruit of me

终结者

你之后我不会再爱别人。不会了，再也不会了
你之后我将安度晚年，重新学习平静
一条河在你脚踝处拐弯，你知道答案
在哪儿，你知道，所有的浪花必死无疑
曾经溃堤的我也会化成畚箕，铁锹，或
你脸颊上的汗水、热泪
我之后你将成为女人中的女人
多少儿女绕膝，多少星宿云集
而河水喧哗，死去的浪花将再度复活
死后如我者，在地底，也将踝骨轻轻挪动

TERMINATOR

After you I shall love no one. No, not another
After you I shall spend my later years in peace, regaining equanimity
When a stream turns at your ankle, you know where
the answer is; you know, all waves are sure to die
The once flooded me shall become a scoop, shovel, or
sweat and tears on your face
After me you shall become the woman of all women
blessed with children, so many like stars gathering
and the stream shouts, and the vanished waves shall resurrect
As dead as I am, even underground, I shall turn the ankle gently

与父亲同眠

夜晚如此漆黑。我们守在这口铁锅中
像还没有来得及被母亲洗干净的两支筷子
再也夹不起任何食物
一个人走了，究竟能带走多少？
我细算着黏附在胃壁里的粉末
大的叫痛苦，小的依旧是

中午时分，我们埋葬了世上最大的那颗土豆
从此，再也不会有人来唠叨了
她说过的话已变成了叶芽，她用过的锄头
已经生锈，还有她生过的火
灭了，当我哆嗦着再次点燃，火
已经从灶膛里转移到了香案上

再也不会有人挨你这么近睡觉了
在漆黑而广阔的乡村夜色中，再也不会
睡得那么沉。我们坚持到了凌晨
我说父亲，让我再陪你一觉吧
话音刚落，就倒在了你腾给我的
空白中

SLEEPING WITH MY FATHER

The night was so dark. We held vigils near the metal wok
like two chopsticks that Mother did not get to wash
no longer able to pick up any food
When a person departs, how much does the person take away
I calculate the particles on my stomach lining
the big ones are called pain, so are the small ones

At noon, we buried the biggest potato in the world
From then on, there would be no more nagging
What she said has already become leaf buds, the hoe she used is
rusty, and the fire she had built
already extinguished. When I reignited the fire, hands trembling, it
already moved from the stove to the incense altar

There will be no one to sleep so close to you
In such a dark and vast country night, you will never sleep
as deeply as you used to. We kept up the vigil till early morning
I said, *father, let me lie down with you one more time*
At these words, I fell down into the place
you freed up for me

我小心触摸着你瘦骨嶙峋的大脚
从你的脚趾上移，依次是你的脚踝和膝盖
最后又返回到自己的胸口
那里，一颗心越跳越快，我听见
狗在窗外狂叫，接着好像认出了来人
悻悻地，哀鸣着，嗅着她

无力拔出人世的脚窝
我又一次颤抖着将手伸向你，却发现
你已经披衣坐在床头。多少漆黑的斑块
从蒙着塑料薄膜的窗口一晃而过
再也没有你熟悉的，再也没有我陌生的
刮锅底的声音

I carefully caressed your big scrawny foot
from the toe upward, to your ankle and then knee
only to return to my own chest
There, my heart beat quicker and quicker. I heard
barking outside the window, as if the dog recognized her
sulkily, mournfully, it sniffled

Caught in the world's rut
I stretched my trembling hands towards you, only to realize
you were already sitting up against the headboard. So many dark apparitions
glided past the plastic film-covered window
yet no more what's familiar to you but strange to me
the sound of wok scraping

信条

1

蒲公英不能长在悬崖上
她恐高，我也恐高
但蒲公英总爱站在悬崖边
风吹她的裙子
风吹她的绒毛
昨晚我从梦中伸出手来
梦里面全是辛苦的味道

2

烧鸡要在绿皮火车上吃
才能唤醒相应的味觉
或者在瑟瑟寒风中
抱紧一坛老酒
躲进桥洞独酌
机帆船开过来了
水手要到船头迎风而尿
然后打个寒噤猫回船舱
方桌上放着一只搪瓷碗
碗里装着花生米
他要用搪瓷杯喝酒
醉意中不停地用手指抠
那几个红字：“为人民服务”
越来越亮的月亮
要从背后照耀
汀面和煤堆
八百里的路上只有我俩
我上溯的时候
你不要动

3

结了冰的脸盆比没结之前沉
你无法将它从记忆中端起
当我哆嗦着回想起
昨晚那盆洗脸水
结了冰的衣服正在铁丝上
冒热气，缓缓位移
太阳照过来了
生活没有改变但生命的
形态发生了变化
僵直的树干指向永恒的天空
弯曲的枝条在河边摇曳
我时而僵直时而弯曲
从冰面上过了河
此后再没有回去过

CREED

1

Dandelion cannot grow on cliffs
She is acrophobic, so am I
But she likes to stand on the edge of a cliff
wind blowing her dress
wind blowing her feathery hair
Last night I extended my hand in my dream
and everything tasted bitter and hard

2

To eat roast chicken, you must do it on a
    green train ride
to activate the corresponding sense of taste
or in howling wind
you must carry a jar of aged liquor
and enjoy it alone under a bridge
The motorized sailboat is coming
The sailor must pee against the wind from the
    deck
tremble and then return, back hunched, to his
    cabin
On the table sits an enamel bowl
inside of which arc peanuts
The sailor must drink liquor with an enamel
    mug
intoxicated his fingers scratching
the red words on the mug: *Serve the people*
The ever-brighter moon
must shine from his back
onto the river surface and coal piles
only seeing you and me on this boat ride of
    hundreds of miles
When I go upstream
you must stay put

3

A frozen basin is heavier than it usually is
You cannot lift it from memory
While I am recalling in shivers
last night's basin of water
the frozen laundry is hanging on the wires
steaming, and shifting its position bit by bit
The sun is shining
Life has not changed
but its state has
Still tree trunks point towards the eternal sky
but bent branches sway along the river
I am stiff in one minute and bent in another
After crossing the river
I have never returned

4

草药在熬过三遍之后
就会淡而无味
我在寡淡的年纪里生过一场大病
我是吃过苦头的人
记忆深处总有一只药罐
歪靠在火笼边
熬药的人是母亲
倒药渣的人是父亲
他们轮流在我身边走来走去
那是此生最寒冷的冬日
雪落在雪上
化成了雪泥
又被雪覆盖
半夜我起来小解
悄悄走到竹林边
查看那堆冷却的药渣
月亮在上
我有一腔苦水
准备留到晚年去吐

5

被喜鹊吵醒的人也会被乌鸦吵醒
高压线上密密麻麻的鸟儿
有时会像一场骤雨
猛然洒向麦地
一个从外地打工回来的人
在公路旁下了车，踌躇着
远远望着位于山坳里的家
他先去屋后看了看菜地
又去门前看了看堰塘里的水
直到所有的活物都被惊动了
才喜忧参半地回到门口
大喊一声：“我回来了！”

6

一头猪在很小的时候就被指定为年猪
它将得到额外的照顾
现在一年到头了
主人要杀它
那天太阳真好
猪在圈中眯眼瞅着墙缝
主人在不远处造灶埋锅
一架喷气式飞机划过长空
一架纸飞机越过杀猪佬
落在了放满刀具的案板上
那是我见过的
最敞亮的乡村生活

4

After three rounds medicinal herbal tea would
taste bland
I got seriously sick when I was at a young and
boring age
I had my share of bitterness
Deep in my memory there was always this jar
laying against our family's hand warmer
My mother made the decoction
my father dumped the dregs
they took turns taking care of me
That was the coldest winter I've experienced
Snow fell on the ground
melted into slush
and then was covered by more snow
At midnight when I got up to pee
I walked to the bamboo grove
to check that pile of cold dreg
The moon above
I was full of bitterness
ready to spit out in my old age

5

Those who could be awakened by magpies
could also be awakened by crows
The birds huddling closely on the powerline
sometimes would suddenly like a downpour
thrust themselves towards the wheat fields
A man returning from his migrant work
got off the bus by the roadside; hesitatingly
he gazed at his family's house in the faraway
valley
He first checked the vegetable fields behind
their house
and then examined the water in the front yard
pond
Until all alive were aroused
did he approach the house's door with mixed
feelings
and announce: "I am home!"

6

At a very tender age the pig was designated to
be the new year pig
which would receive extra care
The year reached the end
and the owner was about to slaughter it
That's a very sunny day
The pig in the pigsty squinted and peeked
through wall cracks
The owner was building a temporary stove
A jet airliner flew across the sky
A paper plane flew past the butcher
and landed on the chopping board full of knives
That's what I've experienced as
the shiniest countryside life

7

河流在等待结冰的季节
两岸的麦地绿油油的
但我们都说麦子很青
青青的麦苗贴着河岸奔跑
而河水早已不再流动
风一遍遍地吹拂沿途的树木
大叶子落完后小叶子落
最小的那片树叶
站在树顶上
一直面朝风的方向

8

每一种作物都是自私的
你看那棵柳树
被各种藤蔓攀附拉扯
结满了南瓜、葫芦、丝瓜和峨眉豆
你看我从母亲胸前
爬到父亲的肩头
去了我能看见的地方
又去了他们看不见的地方

9

秋裤一旦穿上了就不容易脱下
酒后回到床头在黑暗中脱衣服
静电打得你龇牙咧嘴
却照不明她的面容
明天我就要去南方了
穿什么和怎么穿还没有弄清楚

7

When the river was waiting for the icy
season
the wheat fields on both banks were green
which we all called it blue
Green wheat seedlings ran along the
riverbank
while water stopped flowing long ago
Wind repeatedly blew the trees along the way
big leaves fell first, and then smaller ones
The smallest
standing on top of the tree
faced the wind all the time

8

Each crop is selfish
Look at that willow
crawled all over by varied vines
that yield pumpkins, gourds, luffas, and
hyacinth beans
Look at me crawling from my mother's chest
to my father's shoulders
to places I could see
and then to places they could not see

9

Once on long johns are not easy to take off
After drinking I took mine off near my bed in
darkness
Static charges made me grimace in pain
but could not light her countenance
Tomorrow I will head south
What to wear and how to wear it is still a
question

动物之心
——给顶儿

再过几天就是你十六岁的生日
“亲爱的，”早上醒来看见你剩在餐桌上的
半杯牛奶和一堆碎蛋壳，我念叨：亲爱的
这些天，我一直想当面对你说
结果只能默默地
对你杂乱的书桌说
对你塞进洗衣机里的外套说
对你上学的那段水泥路、街道，对你路过的
穷人、富人，对你带动的空气，说
“亲爱的！”
我渐渐变成了一个心口不一的人
一个色厉内荏的人
一个碎嘴的男人——而这恰恰是我
用了四十年时间来反对的
我渐渐变成了我的敌人
亲爱的女儿
终有一天，你也会用恨的方式表达爱意
而这一切
缘于我们都有一颗动物之心

HEART OF AN ANIMAL

—To My Daughter Ding Er

In a few days you will turn sixteen
"My dear," waking up in the morning to see your leftovers on the dinner table
half a bottle of milk and a pile of eggshells, I mumbled: My dear
these days I have been trying to talk with you in person
only ended up saying quietly
to your untidy desk
to the outfit you stuffed into the washing machine
to the concrete road to your school, the streets, people you passed by
poor or rich, and to the air you set in motion; saying
"My dear ! "
I have gradually become one used to saying what I don't think
one that is fierce in appearance but faint in heart
one who nags—which is exactly what I
have been against for the past forty years
I have gradually become my own enemy
Dear daughter
eventually, you will use hate to convey love
and all these are because
we have the heart of an animal

完整的彩虹

完整的彩虹只在纸上出现过
我有纸，你有蜡笔
所以我们应该在一起
完整的生活将被人这样描述:
“穹顶之下，独木难支。”
完整的梦我从来没有完成过
（也许它在梦中是完整的）
我在一场秋雨后醒来
我在天边的一顶帐篷里想象
你钻出帐篷的模样
阳光点燃了你浓密的发梢
天边传来一声惊呼
你危险又安然度过了
又一个完整的夏天

THE PERFECT RAINBOW

The perfect rainbow exists only on paper
I have paper, and you have crayons
so we should be together
The perfect life will be described as
“A lone pillar is unable to hold the firmament”
I have never had a perfect dream
(though it may be perfect in the dream)
I woke up after an autumn rain
and imagined in a tent faraway on the horizon
that you emerge from your tent
the sun lighting up the end of your thick hair
and from the horizon rolling in a loud exclamation
You dangerously yet safely pass
another perfect summer

篇七 一个人本身就是一座城市

VII. *A man in himself is a city.*

张公解梦录

ZHANG'S INTERPRETATION OF DREAMS

梦见牙齿掉了
意味着
我呀我呀我呀
梦见你
从远方跑来
亲吻我
你呀你呀你呀
梦见我都这样了
你居然还是那样子

Dreaming of teeth falling
means
it's me, me, me…
Dreaming of you
running from afar to
kiss me
it's you, you, you…
In dreams I am already like this
yet you somehow remain what you were

黄山松

PINE TREES ON MOUNT HUANGSHAN

从黄山上下来两年后
我又一次想起了
那些高高低低的松树
它们的姿势真的很像烈士
披头散发甚至戴着镣枷
昂首挺胸甚至肩并肩地
站在悬崖边
那天山上起了大雾
我在能见度不足百米的
栈道上慢慢走着，心想
如果我也像它们那样
一动不动地伫立在悬崖旁
你会不会以为我也是
时刻准备为生活就义的人
只是那时我还没有想好
遗嘱。现在我想清楚了：
“那些生活在悬崖边的
肥美的松菌我还没有吃够。”

Two years after climbing Mount Huangshan
I remembered again
its pine trees, both tall and short
Their posture really resembled that of martyrs
gnarled and even shackled
tall and even standing side by side
on the precipices
That day there was fog on the mountain
With nothing visible beyond a hundred meters, I
walked slowly on the plank road, thinking
if I were like the trees
standing perfectly still on a precipice
would I look ready
to sacrifice for life?
By that time I had not come up with a proper
will. Now I have thought it through
Those palatable pine mushrooms near the precipices
I have not had enough of them

深喉 DEEP DESIRE

有没有一只鸟记得你手指的味道	Is there any bird that remembers the taste of your finger?
有没有这样几只雏鸟	Are there baby birds
当你爬上树梢凑近鸟巢	when you got close to their nest
当它们发现你时误以为	they mistook you for their mother
是鸟妈妈衔食归来	back with food
有没有听见叽叽喳喳的叫声	Did you hear their twittering
鹅黄色的喙	Goose yellow beak
深无止境的喉	bottomless throat
你有没有把手指递给它们	Did you extend your finger to them
那是一根少年的手指	the finger of a lad
被每一只雏鸟贪婪地吞咽过	swallowed voraciously by each baby bird
我在中年以后还时常想起	Well into my middle age I still think of
那截温润的指头	that gentle finger
充满了渴望	eager
也探触过最深的渴望	also dabbled into the deepest desire

抹香鲸在睡觉

THE SPERM WHALE IS SLEEPING

我第一次看见抹香鲸在睡觉
一根千年古木倒插
在大海深处
大海在睡觉
我第一次被一个庞然大物的睡姿
感动了——它漂浮
在蔚蓝的梦境里
像婴儿一般漂浮
在母亲的子宫中
阳光从高处插下来像栅栏
维护着抹香鲸
漆黑的身躯
这透明的黑暗
让整座大海忽远忽近

For the first time I saw a sperm whale sleeping
Like an ancient log it stuck vertically
into the deep ocean
that's at sleep
For the first time this gigantic creature's sleeping position
touched me—it floated
on dreamy turquoise waters
like an infant does
in the womb of its mother
Sunbeams thrust down like fences
safeguarding the creature's
pitch-dark body
This transparent darkness
makes the ocean far and near

掰手腕

每一张台面上都有
一对掰手腕的人
每一只手腕都经历过
压迫，抵抗，反转或放弃
当我意识到台面已经撤走
悬在空中的手臂
依然青筋毕暴
依然是这样——我们
拉开了拔河的架势
其实是为了
把自己送入对方的怀抱

ARM WRESTLING

At each table sat
a pair of arm wrestlers
Each wrist has experienced
pressure, resistance, reversal, or renunciation
When I realize the table has gone
my arm remains hanging in the air
veins bulging
It remains like that—We
assume a tug-of-war position
for the actual purpose of
surrendering ourselves to our opponent

老人的力量

POWER OF THE OLD

在夏日的都司湖畔	Summertime at Dusi Lake
层层叠叠的树荫下	in layers of tree shade
老人们三三两两围坐	old folk sit around in twos and threes
有新欢，也有旧仇	new love, long enmity too
但此时他们共沐着一阵风	all bathed in a gust of wind
风从湖面上来	from the surface of the lake
忽冷忽热	blowing hot and cold
像似有若无的琴声	as if faint music sounds
被一架无形的钢琴弹奏	from an invisible piano
能动的手指轻敲膝盖	The abled fingers are lightly tapping kneecaps
能跳的腿脚在石桌下晃动	the bouncy legs and feet are moving about under stone tables
树梢也在晃动	even the treetops are swaying
树荫外面的人匆匆忙忙	People outside the shade are hurriedly
走在阳光里，他们	walking in the sun; they
还得去报恩，或寻仇	need to express gratitude or take revenge
老人们总能从路过的身影中	From the passing figures the old folk would always
看到曾经的我，而现在	be able to spot the former me who by now
我已经被风吹成了人形树	has already been blown into a man-like tree
我的枝丫就分散在他，她	its branches spreading in him, her,
与他们之中	and them

风的意思

立秋以后风还没有进屋的意思
父亲打开门窗却没有纳凉的意思
稻穗饱满，立在田间的稻草人
夸张的双臂没有拥抱的意思
云翳静静地笼罩着池塘
无论荷花是睡是醒也没有离开的意思
但空气在浮动我能感觉到
热浪涂抹在你赤裸的肩胛上
汗珠如壁虎蹑手蹑脚
却没有到达那里的意思

THE INTENT OF THE WIND

After Start of Autumn wind still showed no intent to enter the house
My father kept the door open yet hardly any intent to enjoy cool air
With drooping ears of rice, the scarecrow in the field
displayed no intent to embrace despite its exaggerated long arms
Clouds hovered quietly over the pond, and
awake or asleep, the lotus flowers did not intend to bid farewell
Nonetheless I could feel air moving
Heat waves seeping through your bare shoulder blades
sweat crawled, like a gecko
but did not intend to reach there

松林内外

松鼠把松果埋在了
它自己也找不着的地方
松鼠不停把松果藏起来
像过于孤独的孩子在玩
一个人的迷藏
松鼠和松鼠争抢着
收获，又争相遗忘
冬天已经到了
满地的松针上铺满了雪霜
打雪仗的孩子们躲在松树背后
半张脸被雪团击中
半张脸被寒风涂成酡红
我在松林外面架起了一堆篝火
火焰站起来
它高过了我的头顶
它想逃离灰烬的命运
它想大步流星
至今我还记得那一缕缕松香
欢快的嘶鸣

INSIDE AND OUT OF A PINE FOREST

A squirrel buried pinecones
in a place it could not find later
It hid and continuously hid
like a lonely child playing
solo hide-and-seek
Squirrels fought with each other
for cones, and then forgot the hiding places
Winter already arrived
Pine needles all over the ground were covered by frost
Children who fought with snowballs now hid behind
the pine trees
half of their face hit by snowballs
and the other half flushed by cold wind
I built a bonfire outside the pine forest
The flames flared up
high above my head
eager to escape from fate
and walk in big strides
Now I still remember those wisps of resin scent
and cheerful frolics

一种感觉

把一座水塘的水放干
里面并不见得有鱼
我试过了，你也可以试试
把一座池塘里的水搅浑
也不见得能摸到鱼
每次我把手伸进水里
都能感觉到心跳
而当我每次收回滴水的手掌
我的手指依然半弯曲着
我在乎这种两手空空的感觉
仿佛抓住了
仿佛已然放弃

ONE KIND OF FEELING

Draining a pond
does not necessarily mean a catch
I tried, and you might have a try too
Neither does muddying the water in a pond
necessarily help catch any fish
Each time I put my hand into water
I could feel my own heartbeat
Yet each time I withdrew my dripping hand
my fingers remained half bent
I care much about this emptyhanded feeling
as if I had made it
as if I had let it go

春天来人

SOMEONE COMES IN SPRING

出门遇雨也许不是坏事	Perhaps it's not so bad to walk into rain
有闲情想想去年此时	You have the leisure to recall this moment of last year
你身在何处	where you were
如果去年此时也在下雨	Had it happened to be also a rainy day
不妨想想前年甚至	then go back to the year before or even
更遥远的过去	further past
春雨总有停顿的间隙	Spring rain always takes a hiatus
你站在廊下看屋檐水	In the hallway you'll see raindrops falling from the eave
由粗变细，而河面由浊变清	thick and then thin; and the river, murky and then clear
远山迷濛，裤管空洞	Against faraway mountains, in pant legs empty
有人穿过雨帘走到跟前	someone will walk towards you through the curtain of rain
甩一甩头发露出了	shaking hair from side to side to reveal
一张半生半熟的脸	a face familiar and foreign

油炸荷花

把新鲜的荷花一瓣
一瓣撕下来
蘸上面粉
放进滚烫的油锅里面炸
一望无际的江汉平原
明晃晃的天空下面
采荷花的人继续采荷花
磨面粉的人继续磨面粉
油锅沸腾，你看
滚烫的油水
多么安静

FRIED LOTUS FLOWERS

Tearing off fresh lotus flowers, petal
by petal
dipping them in flour
then frying them in a pan of boiling oil
The Jianghan Plain stretches far and wide
Under the glaring sun
the flower-pickers continue to pick lotus flowers
the millers continue to mill flour
and the oil is sizzling. Lo and behold
the boiling oil looks
so quiet

形色

我下载了一个软件
让它替我辨认
各种各样的生命
以免除我的贫乏和无知
昨天我把镜头对准你
它告诉我你是绣线菊
今天它又说你是关山樱
而当我把镜头对准自己时
它居然说我是：鹤望兰
哦　鹤望兰
多么好听的名字
就像我想你的时候你不是你
就像我想你的时候我不是自己

FORMS

I downloaded an app
to help me identify
variations of life
to avoid being underinformed and ignorant
Yesterday I held the camera towards you
it told me you were a Goldflame spirea
Today it said you were a Kanzan cherry
When I turned the camera towards myself
it actually said I was a bird of paradise
Wow! Bird of paradise
What a beautiful name
Just like you are not you when I miss you
nor am I myself at that moment

和婴儿说话的人

和婴儿说话的人背对我
坐在小花园的条凳上
我以为她在自言自语
走近了才看见她怀抱里的女婴
这是雨后清明的一天
新鲜的树叶在微风中颤栗
我所热爱的世界已经很小了
现在缩成了一个怀抱
我在怀抱外无限眷恋地望着
我在怀抱里“呀呀咿咿”

ONE WHO TALKS TO A BABY

Talking to a baby with her back to me
she sat on a bench in a little garden
I first thought she was talking to herself
until coming closer I saw the baby girl in her arms
That was a clear day after rain
fresh leaves were rustling in a gentle breeze
The world I loved was already pretty small
by then it shrank to that embrace
I watched longingly from outside the embrace
I cooed and babbled inside it

你以为呢

WHAT DO YOU SUPPOSE IT TO BE?

蕙兰开了一月还是谢了
我把凋落的花瓣捡起来
埋在了山茶花盆里
山茶树今年没有开花
越过冬天茎叶枯萎了
我把它连根拔起来
放进了垃圾堆
搁在灶台一角的大蒜发了芽
我把它们埋进了闲置的花盆内
阳光照著绿油油的蒜苗
生也好看
死也不错

The boat orchids wilted after blooming for a month
I picked up the dried up petals
and buried them in the pot of camellia
which did not bloom this year
its leaves and stem withered during the winter
I pulled the shrub by root
and put it into the trash
The garlic placed on a stovetop corner sprouted
I buried it in a spare flower pot
The sun shines on the green sprout
It looks good alive
It's also good after life

数花瓣

COUNTING PETALS

蔷薇的花瓣是恒定的
如果此刻你在蔷薇身边
可以试着数一数
然后转告热爱过她的人
但蔷薇的叶片却不是
我见过无数的落叶和新枝
它们循环在一只花盆周围
那种死去活来的样子
你根本无法描述
有时候我会手持剪刀
走进姹紫嫣红的春天
徘徊在不甘与不舍之间
有时候我会蹲下来想一想
什么是值得我期待的
蓓蕾抿着嘴
忍受了我的絮语
她很难想象这世上的美好
居然都大同小异

The number of rose petals is constant
If you are near a rose
try to count the petals
and then tell whoever loves the flower
Yet the number of rose leaves is different
I have seen countless fallen and fresh leaves
rotate around the flowerpot
their cycle of dying and reviving
simply indescribable
Sometimes scissors in hand I would
walk into a colorful spring
wavering between unable to reconcile and letting go
Sometimes I would squat down and wonder
what is worth expecting
The rose bud purses her lips
tolerating my chattering
She cannot believe wonderful things
are actually alike

在蒸锅旁

BY THE STEAMER

把蟹腿塞进蒸锅
把牢牢抓紧锅沿的蟹腿
使劲往锅里面推
足足花了三分钟
螃蟹们才安静下来
透过玻璃盖
我又一次清晰地看见
这么多的钳螯
在雾气中高举着
当它们慢慢放下来
我也渐渐适应了
用不幸养育幸福

I stuffed all the crab legs into the steamer
For those that held tightly to the steamer's rim
I pushed harder
It took a good three minutes
before the crabs finally quieted down
Through the glass lid
I saw clearly again
so many crab claws
rising high in the steam
When the claws slowly lowered
I also gradually got used to
nourishing the happy with the unfortunate

带绿叶的金钱橘

一只金钱橘
辗转来到我手上
还带着两片叶子
我喜欢娇羞的绿叶
胜过于橘子本身
它让我能想象
那位陌生的采橘人
站在梯子上
头顶蓝天
善解人意

THE KUMQUAT WITH GREEN LEAVES

A Kumquat
after passing through many hands came to me
with two leaves attached
I like the charming leaves
more than the fruit itself
They enable me to imagine
the stranger fruit picker
standing on a ladder
below the sky
and so considerate

一盏明灯

食素的人内心中有一盏明灯
当你对我说：眼前这些
豆制的鸡鸭鱼肉
更合乎生命的本意
我几乎相信了
我原本善类却错生为人
我也几乎看见了我体内
有一片开阔的牧场
我的牛马我的刍狗
正在五台山下，油松林里
残雪覆盖着寺院的屋脊
我拿残躯在大地上蹭来蹭去

THE BRIGHT LIGHT

Vegetarians have an inner bright light
When you told me: All these
chicken, duck, fish and meat made of beans
are more in line with the intent of life
I almost believed
I was kind but wrongly born as a human being
I also almost saw inside me
a vast open pasture
my cows, horses and humble dogs
at the foot of Mount Wutai, or in the red pine forest
Unmelt snow covers the roof of the monastery
and I use my remaining life to nuzzle the vast land

太阳重新升起 THE SUN RISES AGAIN

我曾在故乡的小山顶上	On top of a summit in my hometown I once
目睹过太阳升起的全过程	witnessed the whole process of a sunrise
之前有过很多次	Before that I had done it many more times
之后很少再有这样的机会	Afterwards I seldom had another chance
哪怕是现在我坐在秋阳里	even when I sit in the autumn sun
身体散发出烤红薯的气味	my body emitting the aroma of baked red potatoes
说你爱她，就应憋红了脸再说	To say you love her, you must do it with a crimson face
说过后自己也会面红耳赤	and a flushed you afterwards
再也没有这样的机会了	Never will there be another such chance
当你和我一样远离故乡的山顶	when she and you have gone far from the hometown summit
登完泰山后又来到海边	and have ascended Mount Tai and reached the seaside
说他爱你，就应该云淡风轻	To say you love him, you must do it with calm and ease
你在风中紧拽他的衣襟	You will hold tightly to his lapel in the breeze
大声问：“再说一遍？”	and ask loudly: “Can you say it again?”
而此刻他已经挣扎着跑远	At present he already struggled to run far away
回过头来看见	turning back his head to find
她的头发在燃烧	your hair in a blaze
她的脸你一生只见过一回	your face he had seen only once
之后每一次再见都是重现	and all the later times were mere reappearance

花事

FLOWER AFFAIR

繁忙的季节已经来临
我这里到处都在开花了
你那里也是吧
你身边的人昨天给我打过电话
说起他曾经爱过的人
依然貌美如昨，依然像
那天傍晚我站在樱花树下
看见对面山坡上的那簇梨花
梨花的背后还有桃花
而你在海棠花下
歪着头，捋着一缕缕
先前被人弄乱的长发

The busy season has arrived
Flowers bloom everywhere I go
It must be so on your end too
The one by your side phoned me yesterday
mentioning whom he loved
is still as beautiful as used to be, still like
that cluster of pear blossoms on the hillside across from
where I stood that evening under a cherry tree
Behind the pear blossoms were peach blossoms
but you were under the crabapple blossoms
head tilting, hands twirling strands of
hair tousled by another hand

会笑的人已经不多了

把别人的孩子抱在自己的怀里
先把他弄哭了然后
再把他逗笑——这不是
一件容易的事情
给他看阳光，花朵
摇响你手中的拨浪鼓
给他看你年轻时候的笑容——
这不是抹去皱纹就能够还原的生活
会笑的人已经不多了
会哭的人也是
把别人的孩子抱在自己的胸口
紧紧的
抱着哭
抱住笑
你能给自己的已经越来越少

NOT MANY KNOW HOW TO SMILE ANYMORE

Holding another person's child in arms
to make him first cry
and then laugh—This is not
an easy task
Show him sunshine, and flowers
Shake the rattle in your hand
Share the smiles a younger you once had—
This is not life that can be resumed simply by
smoothing wrinkles
Not many know how to smile anymore
nor to cry
Hold another person's child to your chest
tightly
to cry
to laugh
What you can give yourself is already very little

抱树

三个男孩子合抱一棵银杏
短缺的部分由一位女孩补上
四张脸蛋仰望树梢
四双眼睛顺着树枝往上爬
密密匝匝的银杏叶为他们洒落了一地
为他们曾经有过的
手牵手的
这一日
这棵银杏树年复一年
以相似的模样守候在相同的地方
却再也不见同时出现
在树下的他们
每当落叶季到来的时候
总有人绕树三匝
希望在树后遇见想见的人

HUGGING THE TREE

Three boys tried to hug a ginkgo
The last stretch a girl covered for them
Four faces looked up to the treetop
Four pair of eyes climbed upwards
Thick ginkgo leaves covered the ground
for the boys and the girl had once had
hand in hand
such a day
Year after year the tree
would wait in the same spot with a similar pose
yet it never witnessed again the appearance
of the four under itself
Whenever the tree started to drop leaves
someone would walk around it three times
in hopes of meeting the longed-for

在雨天睡觉

我能把握的幸福已经少之又少
在雨天睡觉算是一种
窗外大雨瓢泼
我已经醒来却还在等待
另外一个梦成型
哪怕再也无法入睡
只是闭上眼心平气和地
想一想：我与他们
有什么不一样？有什么
是我行至人生中途还能把握的
云团挣脱天空
雨点收不住脚
来到大地上的事物相互混淆
我已经有过长久的浑浊
现在我想变得清澈些
就像现在这样
窗外在下雨
看样子还会下下去
这大概就是你说的幸福
我能预感某张亲切的脸
正从虚掩着的门缝里看我
却不惊扰我

SLEEP ON A RAINY DAY

The happiness I can assure for myself is already paltry
Sleeping on a rainy day counts as one kind
Outside the window it pours cats and dogs
I am awake but still waiting
for another dream to take shape
even though I may not fall asleep again
and I may only close my eyes and calmly
think: Between them and me
what's the difference? What is it
that I can still hold onto at this stage of my life
Clouds have struggled free from the sky
and raindrops cannot stop falling
All things on earth have mixed up
I have wallowed in turbidity
and now I aspire to be clearer
just like it is now
Outside the window it is raining
and it will continue to rain
This is what you call happiness
I can feel an amicable face
is looking at me from the crack of the door
yet not disturbing me

家宴

酒后才想起
昨晚是在自家吃的饭
经验之一
多请女性家宴因为
她们走后家里干净得
好像没有来过人
教训之一
先饮白酒后喝啤
昨晚我搞反了
不是繁星宴请了夜空
而是夜空宴请了繁星

FAMILY BANQUET

After the hangover
did I realize last evening's dinner was at my place
One practice to keep
to invite female guests more often because
after they leave the house is so clean
as if nobody were there
One lesson to learn
First alcohol and then beer
I did it the reverse order last night
not the stars invited the night sky
but the other way around

一滴汗珠

被我格外珍惜的一滴汗珠
此刻正滚过我的胸口
接下来它将经过我中年微凸的
腹部，凹陷的肚脐，和下腹
我并不清楚它的夏日之旅
将在何处终结
我只是静静地感受它的蠕动
那么轻柔，酥痒，而欢快
我已经很久没有这样专注过了
因为一滴汗珠
让我沉醉在对肉体的审视中
现在它越过了我的腹部
像一个晶莹剔透的少年
翻过山坡来到路边
一间油毛毡棚旁
巨大的烈日炙烤着
他那颗刚刚浮出水面的光头
河水在不远处闪光
河流在远处不知去向

A DROP OF SWEAT

A drop of sweat much treasured by me
is rolling past my chest
about to pass my middle-aged slightly bulging
stomach, sunken belly button, and lower abdomen
I am not sure where its summer trip
will come to an end
I just quietly enjoy its slithering movement
so gentle, tickling, and joyful
I've not been so concentrated for long
over a drop of sweat
indulging myself in contemplating the corporeal
Now the sweat has crossed my belly
like a crystal-clear youngster
climbed over the slope and reached
a roadside linoleum tent
The huge scorching sun bakes
his bare dome that just floated to the water's surface
water sparkling nearby
river disappearing far away

钨丝的战栗

从前的灯泡比现在亮多了
从前的白日里面塞满了梦境
农具挂在墙壁上
屋檐下垂着蒜瓣和高粱穗
从前的风也不像现在这样吹
摇摆的灯绳来回摇摆
少年走过去扯一下
少女的眼睛就发光
从前我长时间坐在黑暗中
屏住呼吸倾听电流在体内涌动
外面的脚步声到了哪儿
哪里就开始战栗

VIBRATION OF THE TUNGSTEN FILAMENT

Light bulbs used to be much brighter
Days used to teem with dreams
Farm tools were hung on walls
garlic and sorghum bunches under the eaves
Wind used to blow differently too
The pull string swung back and forth
The young man walked over and pulled it
and the eyes of the young woman glowed
I used to sit in darkness for long durations
holding my breath to feel electric currents surging
    through my body
Outside the room wherever the feet moved
that's where vibrations took place

手机里的菩萨

从云冈石窟出来
手机里多出了很多尊菩萨
在去往雁门关的路上
我一路翻看着他们的情貌
痛苦被放大了
欢乐被缩小
菩萨啊，这么多的砂岩之躯
任由岁月涂抹
这么多的残肢
依然在行走、抚摸和讲述
而我独爱最小的那一窟
他像我小时候
不谙世事
以为哭泣就能得到所求
以为欢笑就能满足所有

BODHISATTVA IN MY CELLPHONE

By the time I departed Yungang Grottoes
many bodhisattvas found home in my cellphone
On the way to Yanmen Pass
I flipped the photos and examined them
sufferings magnified
joy minimized
Oh, Bodhisattva! So many bodies of sandstone
abraded by years
So many broken limbs
still walk, caress, and tell tales
Yet, I was only fond of that smallest one
like the younger me
ignorant of the world
he believes crying leads to prayers answered
and laughter satisfies all there are

雪里红

我喜欢所有来历明确的事物
来自安徽枞阳的白皮小罗卜
来自恩施、长阳或兴山的榨辣椒
岩耳来自巴东
冲菜来自远安
板栗来自罗田
白菜薹从我老家来
带着荆门的雨水和泥土
——我喜欢前天傍晚时分
西天云破处的那点太阳
那几缕闪现在乌云周围的金光
突然让我想到了雪里红
不知道哪里的雪里红
比我小时候吃过的更好
更像雪里红——像放学归来
不放书包就直奔厨房
揭开桌罩的那个小女生

MUSTARD GREEN, AKA XUE LI HONG

I like all things of a clear origin
white radishes from Zongyang, Anhui
pickled chili crisp from Enshi, Changyang or Xingshan
rock ear from Badong
preserved mustard from yuan'an
chestnuts from Luotian
flowering cabbage from my hometown
tasting of rain and soil of Jingmen
—I like the dusk of the day before yesterday
with sunburst through the clouds in the western sky
The rays of gold accenting the edge of the clouds
suddenly reminded me of Xue Li Hong
out of nowhere
tasting better than what I had in childhood
more mustard green than mustard green—like that
after-school
girl, satchel still on one shoulder, yet already rushing to
the kitchen
to open the food tent cover

乌龟之徒

一只乌龟从雨后的柴垛里
爬出来，举着可笑的脑袋
在它到达目的地之前
没有人知道它的目的
一只乌龟缩在我的记忆深处
它一动不动的时候
我的记忆一片沉寂
晚霞收敛于一朵蘑菇上
蘑菇会在夜晚生长
乌龟也会在黑暗中爬行
那一年我并没有生活
我在生病，求生的欲望
让我在夜晚依然竖着耳朵
谛听人世的动静
一只乌龟从黑暗中爬出来
光明让它既爱又恨
它慌不择路的时候
我正走在胡乱求医的路上
那时候的天空真是蓝啊
乌龟举着脑袋
慈祥地看着
病中的我

TURTLE TREK

After the rain from the firewood pile
crawls out a turtle, holding its funny head high
Until it reaches its destination
nobody knows where it is heading
The turtle that crouches deep in my memory
when motionless
my memory is silent
The evening glow hovers over a mushroom
which will grow during the night
The turtle can crawl in darkness too
That year I did not have a life
I was sick; the desire to survive
prompted me to stay alert even at night
for any movements in the world
The turtle crawled out of darkness
It loved brightness as much as it hated it
When it panicked
I was on the way to see my doctor
The sky was so azure that
the turtle raised its head
and looked lovingly
at me the sick boy

自行车的故事

从前有一位女孩
总爱坐在自行车的后座上
铃铛响亮
裙摆里面装满了风
从前有一辆自行车
后座上总是坐着这位女孩
其他的自行车都环绕着它
从宽阔的操场到拥挤的马路
所有的车都迷失了方向
春天到了郊外
山坡上开满了杜鹃
所有的自行车都从城里驶出来
铃铛一路响啊，直到这位女孩
从后座上来到了前杆上
插满杜鹃花的自行车队
静静地擦过了那个春天

A BIKE STORY

Once there was a girl
who loved to sit on the back of a bike
Its bell rang loud and clear
Her skirt billowed out with breeze
Once there was a bike
on whose back seat the girl always sat
The other bikes circled it
from spacious playground to crowded streets
All the bikes lost their direction
Spring came to the outskirts
where azaleas bloomed over hills
The bikes departed the city
their bells ringing until the girl
moved from the back to the front bar
The bikes bedecked with azaleas
quietly brushed against that spring

天太凉了有点冷

从北方来的云遇到从南方来的云
它们在天上推推攘攘
它们是我最早见过的大象、老虎和神
已经下过雨了
风把树叶掀开就能看见杏子、桃子和李子
我从一棵树上蹿到另一棵树上
我在变幻的云朵下面模拟过
一切遥远之物的影子
神秘的不是它们，是我自己

IT'S GETTING COOL OR EVEN COLD

Clouds from the north met those from the south
pushing and shoving each other
They were the first elephants, tigers, and gods I saw
It had rained
and wind blew about leaves to reveal apricots, peaches, and plums
I hopped from one tree to another
simulating under the clouds
shadows of all faraway things
What's mysterious was not them, but me

慢动作

所有的慢动作都好看——
绿芽慢慢拱出泥土
花苞慢慢打开
花瓣边落边在风中旋转
涧溪得过且过，而蝌蚪
在尾巴脱落的瞬间
趾蹼才分出了清水与浊流
——这些慢啊，这
所有的慢
都抵不上从道路尽头
缓缓驶来的那辆轮车
轮辐在朝阳里闪闪发光
当我们看清楚它的时候
它已经沉浸在了晚霞中
而此时你我在熙攘的街头
像所有人一样擦身而过
我回头看过你了
但你没有看我
你回头看我的时候
我假装骄傲地消逝在了人群中
然后你上了你的轮车
我下了我的坡道
我慢慢活成了我，活成了
你再也不想见到的那一个

SLOW MOTION

All slow motions look great—
Green seedlings growing slowly out of soil
flower buds unfolding gradually
petals swirling in the air while falling
mountain streams muddling along, tadpoles
at tail losing moment
their webbed feet finally telling clear water from
    muddy
—their slow motions, all
these slow motions
are nothing compared with that end-of-the-road
slow-moving of a vehicle
its spokes shining in the rising sun
and in full view
it being already bathed in the setting sun
For then among the bustling street crowd
you and I passed by like all others did
I turned to look at you
but you paid me no attention
When you turned to look at me
I disappeared with false pride in the crowd
Then you boarded your vehicle
and I walked down the slope
Step by step I've lived to become me,
    becoming one
you never want to meet again

清晨的鱼汤

请过来喝一碗鱼汤
它由各种鱼混合在一起
通宵熬成，浓稠，鲜美
带有晨雾的甜腥味
请过来帮我
把灶膛里的余烬熄灭
用你那双从来不曾触碰过
柴火的手触碰一下
从灰烬中浮现出来的妻儿
幸存者的每一天都该受到祝福
谁先醒来谁就是领受者
活着是一桩见者有份的事业
死亡也是，既然如此
请你慢慢凑近这口祖传的大锅
我已经将盛满鱼汤的碗搁置
在每一条必由之路上
路过的人请端起它
放心喝下
晨雾在散去
好日子如鲠在喉
请把空碗倒扣
在我经过的每一条路旁

FISH SOUP FOR THE MORNING

Please come to enjoy a bowl of fish soup
It's a mixture of all sorts of fish meat
simmered overnight, thick, delicious
and tinged with the sweet fishy flavor of morning mist
Please come to assist me in
putting off the last embers in the stove
and with your hands that have never touched
firewood to touch
the visage of your wife and child in ashes
Survivors should be blessed each day
Whoever wakes up first receives the blessing first
To stay alive is the cause all survivors share
So does the cause to die. If so
please come slowly to this ancestral wok
I have already placed bowls of fish soup
along all the roads to be traveled
Whoever comes by do have a bowl
sip and be assured that
the morning mist will disperse
and good life is at the throat
Please place your empty bowl upside down
along all roads I will embark on

鸣 谢

这本书完成离不开很多人的支持和帮助。在此特别感谢我的同事布莱恩·彼特斯（Bryan L. Peters）教授对初稿的慷慨反馈。诗人张执浩老师信任我，授予我翻译许可；我的编辑李黎老师细心而专业；我的老朋友李红博士不仅热爱诗歌，还十分支持我。这里一并感谢他们。当然最后还要感谢我的家人，他们不断给我鼓励、支持和爱。

本书有些译文首次发表于各种英语出版物，有些略有改动，具体情况如下：

- 《逆行》首发于《阿姆斯特丹评论》2024 年秋季
- 《蟑螂想不明白》和《翠鸟的一天》首发于《敏锐》, 2024 年 5 月，第 109 期
- 《锦鲤》《原来是这样》《仿〈枕草子〉》和《一只蚂蚁出门了》首发于《闪避》, 2024 年 4 月
- 《秋葵》《把手伸进别人的兜里》《像样的爱情》和《红桦树》首发于《德洛斯：翻译与世界文学》, 2023 年第 2 期，总第 38 卷
- 《如果根茎能说话》《冬青树》和《茄子》首发于《铜镍》，2023 年第 36 期
- 《滚铁环》《夜晚的习惯》《咏春调》和《答枕边人，兼致新年》首发于《今日中国文学与思想》，2022 年春，第 3 卷，1-2 期合刊
- 《南瓜诗》首发于《蓝果树季刊》，2022 年第 27 期
- 《无主之树》首发于《虎蛾评论》，2022 年 9 月，第 8 期

- 《万古烧》《跳出油锅的鱼》《在蒸锅旁》《油炸荷花》和《花饭》首发于《译丛》, 2022 年春，第 97 期
- 《今年的最后一首诗 , 2019》首发于《第 91 条子午线》，2021 年 5 月
- 《在一起》首发于《交流》，2021 年 5 月 8 号
- 《自行车的故事》于 2021 年 3 月首次刊载于何跃敏和李红主持的一个微信公众号

ACKNOWLEDGEMENTS

This poetry translation book would not have been possible without the help of many. Special thanks to my colleague and English professor Bryan L. Peters for his generous feedback; to my editor Li Li for her expert editing and meticulous guidance; to poet Zhang Zhihao who gave me permissions to translate his poems; to my long-term friend and poetry lover Dr. Li Hong for her remarkable support and interest; and last but not least to for their encouragement, support and love.

Grateful acknowledgement is made to the editors of the following publications in which these poems, sometimes in slightly modified versions, first appeared:

- "Walk Towards Each Other" in *Amsterdam Review* (Fall 2024)
- "Cockroaches Cannot Understand" and "A Day of the Kingfisher" in *Acumen*, 109 (May 2024)
- "Koi Fish," "So That's How It's Got to Be," "In the Style of *The Pillow Book*," and "An Ant Ventured Out" in *The Dodge* (April 15, 2024)
- "Okra," "Putting Your Hand in Someone's Pocket," "Heart on Fire," and "Red Birch" in *Delos: A Journal of Translation and World Literature* (vol. 38, iss. 2, 2023)
- "If the Root Could Speak," "The Holly Tree," and "Eggplant" in *Copper Nickel* 36 (2023)

- "Hoop Rolling," "Night Habit," "To the Tune of Spring," and "In Response to My Love, To the New Year as Well" in *Chinese Literature and Thought Today* 3, no.1–2 (Spring 2022)
- "Song of the Pumpkin" in *Tupelo Quarterly* 27 (2022)
- "Nobody's Tree" in *The Tiger Moth Review* 8 (September 21, 2022)
- "The Everlasting Pot," "Fish That Jumped Out of the Oil Pan," "By the Steamer," "Fried Lotus Flowers," and "Fried Rice" in *Renditions* 97 (Spring 2022)
- "End of the Year Poem, 2019" in *91st Meridian* (May 8, 2021)
- "Together" in *Exchanges* (May 8, 2021)
- "A Bike Story" was shared on an online post hosted by He Yuemin and Li Hong (March 19, 2021)

BIBLIOGRAPHY

Barash, David P. *Buddhist Biology: Ancient Eastern Wisdom Meets Modern Western Science.* Oxford: Oxford University Press, 2013.

Ingram, Paul O., and David R. Loy. "The Self and Suffering: A Buddhist-Christian Conversation." *Dialog: A Journal of Theology* 44. 1 (Spring 2005): 98-107.

Wu, Fusheng. "From Scripture to Literature: Translations of the Shijing by James Legge and Arthur Waley." *History Retold: Premodern Chinese Texts in Western Translation*, edited by Leo Tak-hung Chan and Zong-qi Cai, Brill, 2022, pp. 90-117.

Zhang Zhihao. "I Have Seen the Yellow Crane." *Reading Poetry Under the Yellow Crane Tower.* Wuhan: Changjiang Literature and Art Publishing House, 2022. pp. 271-308.

—. "Poets' Music Register" ("Shirenmen de yinqu"). *Shi shouhuo (Poetry Harvest),* Summer 2022, pp. 244-250.

后 记

翻译诗人张执浩的作品缘起于六年前，那时我和一位朋友已经翻译《诗经》多年。我们每周翻译一首，然后互相对比、交流、提高。译了几十首《国风》和《小雅》后，我认为应该译一些当代诗歌，贴近当下的生活。于是我们浏览阅读了不少现当代诗人的作品。其中张执浩诗歌的风格，我甚是喜爱。出书的想法源于给学生开写作课 。这本书因此是我以一个语言文学研究教育者的热忱选编、翻译、和结集的。

张执浩的诗专注普通人的日常生活，简洁流畅，又极具启发性。不管是乡村还是城镇，过去还是现在，也不管是个人还是间接触及的人生经历，他的处理都得心应手，游刃有余。 这和诗人遵循“目击成诗”的古训有关。他总能从日常细节入手，低入高出，引领读者到入胜之处。比方说，在《一杆秤》里，我们先看见一群嬉笑打闹的调皮乡村玩童，稍后体味的是一位成人的柔软内心，最后领悟的是人对周遭事物想当然的傲慢及生而为人的秉性 。大多数读者毕竟都喜欢故事，也乐于参与“始于欢愉、终于智慧”（罗伯特・弗罗斯 /Robert Frost）的语言游戏。又比如《左对齐》中，叙述者一边带我们在纸上行走，追逐摸索语言奇迹，一边又助我们神游远方蓝天白云下的家园。寥寥几行诗句或唤醒我们美好的记忆和惆怅，或令我们眼界大开，或让诗歌这个小众的艺术瞬间产生强烈的感染力。诗人融情于事，叙事及情的写作无疑是成功的。

平易又有诗意，貌似容易，实则需要很强的对生活和语言的敏感，知识消化、储存和转换的技巧，洞察宇宙和人世宽阔的悟性，以及天赋和对诗歌这个“大家伙”（张执浩）的执念。作为译者，我尽量做一个忠实的“双胞胎”（格雷戈里・帕

尔德罗 / Gregory Pardlo ），全面体现原作各方面的魅力，包括其语境、内涵外延、句式措词、修辞、音乐性等等。同时我坚信好的诗歌翻译本身也是独立的艺术创作，既能保持原作的精髓光华，又能反映移入语言和文化的特点、习惯、和接受方式，甚至译者自有的创意和风格。当读者在翻阅中捕捉到我为之而努力的各种细微表现，并欣然互动 ，当读者看到这些诗从一个语言家乡迁入到另一个语言新居，演绎新的生命过程，且为之敞开心扉，这本书就实现了初衷。

何跃敏

2024 年 7 月

图书在版编目（CIP）数据

我见过黄鹤：汉、英 / 张执浩著. -- 北京：外文出版社，2024. 9. -- ISBN 978-7-119-14025-4

Ⅰ. I227

中国国家版本馆 CIP 数据核字第 2024XQ9184 号

责任编辑：李　黎
英文翻译：何跃敏
英文改稿：Bryan L. Peters
英文审读：吴礼敬
装帧设计：祁泽娟
内文排版：邱　彬
印刷监制：章云天

我见过黄鹤

张执浩 著　　何跃敏 译

出 版 人：胡开敏
出版发行：外文出版社有限责任公司
地　　址：中国北京西城区百万庄大街 24 号　　**邮政编码：**100037
网　　址：http://www.flp.com.cn　　**电子邮箱：**flp@cipg.org.cn
电　　话：008610-68320579（总编室）　008610-68996182（编辑部）
008610-68995852（发行部）
制　　版：北京青侣文化创意设计有限公司
印　　刷：艺堂印刷（天津）有限公司
开　　本：700mm×1000mm　1/16
装　　别：精装
印　　张：16
版　　次：2024 年 9 月第 1 版第 1 次印刷
书　　号：ISBN 978-7-119-14025-4
定　　价：98.00 元